BLITZ

WE PLAY TO WIN THE GAME

Demetrius Jones x DC Hicks

No part of this publication may be reproduced, distributed, or transmitted in any form or by any means, including photocopying, recording, or other electronic or mechanical methods, without the prior written permission of the publisher, except in the case of brief quotations embodied in reviews and certain other non-commercial uses permitted by copyright law.

Copyright © 2023 by Demetrius Jones

All rights reserved.

Printed in the United States of America.

ISBN 978-1-958294-09-3 (paperback)

Library of Congress Control Number: 2022923120

Published by ABOOKFELLOFFATRUCK, LLC
Detroit, Michigan

abookfelloffatruck.com
aboxfelloffatruck

DEDICATION

This book is dedicated to all the women, all the men, all the people that never got an opportunity to pursue their passion, life calling, or dreams due to the patriarchy, white supremacy, classism, sexism or discrimination.

May you be blessed to share the world with someone like University of Tennessee Lady Vols Head Coach Pat Summit. Accruing over 1,098 career wins, the most in college basketball history at the time of her retirement. Her coaching style was based on confronting shortcomings and failures through a balance of honesty and sympathy. It inspired this book and showed us all what we can be if given a chance.

May you be fortunate to live in the times of people like Dawn Staley and Angela O'Neal who showed me how difficult it can be for women to get an opportunity.

May you be felicitous enough to be befriended by voracious readers like Dr. Amber Burnette who force you through their enthusiasm to fall in love with fiction.

May you be favored and have a friend like Damon Brock who showed me the importance of mentors through his patience, unselfishness, and friendship in teaching me how to play and love Madden. Not only did you teach me but you were so open, you never dreamed of me becoming better than you. And you also never once expressed a scintilla of regret.

May you be lucky enough to have a mom with as much ambition and drive as Carolyn Jones, so that you are inspired to reach light years beyond your grasp despite the forces in your way.

But if the Universe fails to create more of these wonderful humans I pray it has guided my hand during each keystroke. Pray that somehow I managed to paint lines of prose that capture a semblance of the inspiration, wisdom, love, and knowledge imparted to me. Pray that I have given you something to help yourself and others in our struggle to dismantle the patriarchy, white supremacy, classism, sexism and discrimination.

ACKNOWLEDGMENTS

Special thanks, appreciation, praise, and gratitude to my uber talented co-writer Donna Hicks. Together we used our spirits and technology to do the impossible. Together we imagined a better future. Together we created a better world.

Thank you to my editor Dr. Erin Macri. If it is possible, you are a being of pure intelligence and heart. You both gave unselfishly to this project. Thank you for using your super powers to make this bit of prose something special. Your talent is a celestial force.

Thank you Tanya Maifat! You are an artistic genius!

Thank you Mom and Dad for always encouraging me in all my endeavors. Special thanks to Mom for attending all my talent shows. Seeing your face during my life's best moments made them so. When your parents support your dreams with love it is impossible for the world to ever take them away with any amount of hate.

"People who work together will win, whether it be against complex football defenses, or the problems of modern society."
~ Vince Lombardi, Head Coach Green Bay Packers

Gouge the eyes. Crush the windpipe. Mangle the groin. Time is the final frontier. Like two couples, double-date walking into a restaurant, these four thoughts entered her mind at once. Not necessarily in this order. She could have thought to mangle the groin, crush the windpipe, and then gouge the eyes. When one believes they are under attack, details get lost. But 30 years from the moment, thinking back she would always remember that gouge the eyes was the last thought. That said, *time is the final frontier* stuck. As in most conflicts, time was the most important variable. If she only had a few seconds longer, she could decide whether it would be more gratifying to blind, suffocate, or sterilize the man in front of her rather than to answer his question.

"Are you Cleo White?"

After hearing the question a second time, Cleo's forward momentum came to an abrupt halt. Cleo watched Tip running his eyes across her in study from head to toe. As he took in her every molecule, she followed those judgy pupils and knew his every thought. Though his Double Windsor Knot deportment suggested he was an upstanding, distinguished gentleman, Cleo knew his type, rich, elitist, and patriarchal af.

She smirked, thinking of how he likely assigned her a rating of seven on a scale of one to ten. Well, 7–8. He was the type to run a range. If he knew she was 26, she might lose a few points because she was closer to 30 than to 21. His opinion didn't scare her. Whatever he thought about her, she at one time or another had thought worse.

If he thought her brown hair should be blonde, no problem because so had she. If he thought her 5'4 ½ length should have been 5'10, so had she. And yes, she wanted that 1/2, it was hers so she claimed it. If he thought her hazel eyes should be emerald, so had she. White and pale, rom-com best friend and sidekick, vertically challenged, so had she, so had she, so had she. In her mind, in her world, without trying, she was just cute enough not to be pretty.

But effort? Only someone that wanted something would put in the effort to bring out their beauty. An unofficial genetic lottery winner, Cleo had a well-proportioned Hollywood starlet type of body that if given access to the canon of fashion would look good in absolutely anything. However, she purposefully made it hard to find it by covering it in the frumpiest of frumpy clothing. Goal weight? Cleo was happy with each of her 130 lbs.

She simply didn't feel like being beautiful. She knew if she put in the effort, her hair was thick and radiant enough for ads. Her eyelashes were the type that drag-queens would kill for but her unarched eyebrows, dry skin, chapped lips, and slight face stache galleried canvas that she thought only a pimp could love.

In short, she was an above average-looking white girl with the face symmetry of a perfectly cut jewel. Her lips formed a marquise diamond spaced one and a half kisses from a jasper pendant nose and sapphire doe eyes. Hard and soft at the same time, she was a perfect equation of possible gorgeousness, a treasure waiting to be discovered or unlocked. She wasn't ready to do the math or excavation. But once she smiled, you saw it, yes it, pretty girl swag. That swag inside her was her greatest asset. Cleo had the capacity to be a superhero or super villain. For now, she was changing the world. Too bad for Tip that he had traded in the currency of actuality, instead of the coin of potential.

Who was this five to judge her?

With her mouth slightly agape, she eyed the strange man standing in front of her. Wearing a three-piece suit and dark sunglasses, he looked in his late sixties, though if she had to guess, he was probably actually somewhere in his mid-fifties. Everything about him screamed government official—at least as they were so often portrayed on Netflix. He was the type to judge women for every extra ounce beyond his fantasy female weight allowance, meanwhile making every excuse for the perfectly acceptable extra 20 pounds he was toting. And that was strike one for Tip in Cleo's eyes or rather a flag on the play. Hypocrite!

What did he want from her? She couldn't decide. Her eyes dropped to his midsection looking for some sort of concealed weapon. Taser? Burner? Nope. Instead she discovered the beginnings of a middle-age spread. By the looks of him, she surmised that he had skipped more than a few workouts and replaced them with Taco Tuesdays.

Never skip a leg day.

Cleo figured that if she decided to run, the odds were in her favor. She was standing on a concrete island/park of sorts on the riverfront of downtown Detroit. Blocked from traffic, save one side of the street that allowed for drop-off, pick up, and short conversations. If you were crying that day and your tears landed on the right eye lashes, Hart Plaza looked like a European square.

A town square by American but not European standards, it drew as much attention as its art installations, including the 24-foot-long arm with a fisted hand suspended by a 24-foot-high pyramid framework created by Robert Graham. Essentially a floating fist surprisingly (or unsurprisingly, depending on who you asked) called The Fist.

The Fist was dedicated to social activist heavyweight boxing champion from 1937-1950, Joe Louis, hailed as "America's first Black national hero". The statue was both celebrated and vilified as a symbol of Black Power. In this debate, Cleo was definitely one of the party people. She always found that moniker, "America's first Black national hero," odd given that Crispus Attucks, a Black man, had been the first person to die in America's war for independence, the American Revolution.

And as if that wasn't strange enough, after The Fist was built, the City went on to build a second statue—this time of Joe Louis' whole body—in another part of Detroit. Why? Cleo would not have believed it had her parents not been in attendance at the meeting where outcries were heard from the citizens of Detroit. Despite the fact that The Fist had been a gift from *Sports Illustrated*, citizens actually thought The Fist stopped at the elbow only because the City of Detroit had run out of money and stopped building it.

Cleo's efforts to know things like this and to empathize with those who thought things like this provided her two paths in life, both equally dangerous. She would either be a saint or sinner that could move effortlessly between groups regardless of race, class, gender, or philosophy. Today, thanks to her saintlier efforts as a community organizer of two simultaneous Hart Plaza protests, the Plaza was jam packed with activists. If the man before her, or anyone else for that matter, pursued her, they would bump into other people every two or three steps, and meet a fist similar to The Fist pointed at Canada.

If only it was raining rather than beaming sunshine, she would have a guaranteed getaway given her choice of fashionable fleeing footwear. Mind you, she had chosen this sparsely tree-lined concrete plaza nestled between the Detroit River, General Motors Headquarters, and TCF Center because she had been chased—and had chased others—six or seven times before. Her getaway record was 3-0.

Those chases had taken place long ago, way back when

Hart Plaza was still the site for a variety of ethnic festivals ranging from the African-American Festival to the Honky Tonk Festival. It always made Cleo chuckle when she noticed that all the T-shirt, accessory, and keepsake vendors at the African-American Festival were also at the African Festival, the Blues Festival, the R & B Festival, and the BBQ Festival but never at the Country Music Festival.

Amongst the shea butters, African art and designer replicas, Cleo even found a real Calvin Klein mood watch with a face that changed color. Though it was priced at $10, she had used all the negotiation and business skills she had accumulated over her 14 years on planet earth to talk the vendor down to $5. It had helped that all she had was $5 that she had found on her way to the festival.

That same watch still rested on her wrist today, right now, as she pondered her next move. The watch reminded her of the hope of escape. Much like the art sculpture to her left did, because it looked remarkably like a replica of the Stargate, a portal that could transport a person to other worlds. Much like the monument behind her did, reminding passersby that the plaza had once been a part of the Underground railroad, allowing escaping Africans to flee to Canada.

The weight of all these symbols of escape was not lost on her. While she considered whether or not she wanted to spend the rest of her days as a fugitive of the law, she stole a discreet glance around her shoulder. Hushed murmurs could be heard rolling through the crowd.

The counterfeit calm was as deceptive as it was honest. It was the same kind of calm that makes the air feel unnaturally heavy right before a tornado touches down. Like the awkward silence on a suburban-only SMART bus that does not pick up passengers in Detroit, when someone says something racist to another passenger, and everyone hears it but not a soul moves.

Cleo was close to betting that it was too noisy for the admirers of gothic skyscrapers to hear Tip's cries of pain. She was guessing even if engaged in combat, they were just far enough away from those enjoying the street art installations or those protesting for anyone to see her unleash the black cloud of whoop-ass inside her.

Standing on the edge of the storm, visions of her face trending on the IG discovery section accompanied by the obligatory FBI Most Wanted hashtags filled her mind. Endless days and nights drifting from one seedy motel room to the next…

"Fine… it was me," Cleo called out.

"So, you are Cleo White?" the man reaffirmed.

"Yes… yes. I did it! And I would gladly do it again. Do you have any idea how many innocent animals are killed in this country because of this barbaric industry?"

"The harder you WORK, the harder it is to SURRENDER."
~ Marv Levy, Buffalo Bills

The man pulled his sunglasses down his nose and gave her a thoughtful expression. After a moment, he shrugged. "No, actually I don't. Do you know?"

Cleo's mouth opened and closed. "Well… I don't know the specific number, but I know it's in the thousands."

"Really," Tip nodded. "It's kind of cruel though."

"Exactly."

"No, I mean playing a numbers game with a numbers guy and not knowing the exact number," Tip explained.

"What?" Cleo gasped with outrage. "I should have known you wouldn't understand."

"It was her," a loud female voice yelled out from somewhere behind her.

Cleo's righteous indignation was replaced by an ice-cold lump of dread that filled her belly. In slow motion, she turned to see a crowd parting almost biblical in proportion. When the last of the throng of supporters fell away, Cleo saw two very angry animal killers. Both were clutching their high heels in one hand and their paint splattered fur coats in the other, and both were eyeing her down like she was about to be their next meal.

Whirling back towards the so-called numbers man, Cleo announced, "Enough playing around. Take me to Gitmo or whatever black site it is you take people like me to."

"Gitmo? Black site?" Tip chuckled as he retrieved his wallet from his vest. "I was thinking more along the lines of Ford Field," he explained as he flashed his work badge. "NFL, not FBI. Both have three letters but our jobs are slightly different."

Tip motioned with his hand, warlock. Cleo glanced around, skeptic. Though moments ago she was confident she could maim Tip as he was out of shape and therefore light work, her "spidey sense" was sending her a warning that something was different about this new threat. Maybe it was the realization that the two women were moving towards her at a level seven elliptical machine speed. Or maybe it was the fact that she did not know if it was their anger or cardio endurance training that allowed them to move so surely while barefooted. Either way it did not bode well for her.

As if by magic, a black stretch Mercedes-Maybach pulled to a stop at the curb in front of them. By even greater sorcery, the door opened on its own accord. Cleo leaned down and spied a young attractive man sitting inside. Engrossed in the television program that was playing from the screen that looked as if it was forged inside the middle console, he was completely oblivious to the commotion outside.

"Who is that? Your servant?" Cleo asked.

Without complimenting his servant's prompt arrival, Tip halfway placed his body into the vehicle. He did so with the hurried grace of someone late for an "everything is fine" meeting where running would set off alarms that, "everything was not fine" but he needed to run because otherwise things would not be fine.

In that situation Tip was the type to run, then stop when he saw someone, say good morning, afternoon, or evening like it was copacetic then break out into a full sprint. That was Tip—cool and calculated as a garter snake eyeing its last chance at getting the prey before winter.

"We call them personal assistants these days but... his name is Curtis, and I am Tip McMann. Your time clock has nearly reached the end. Are you coming?"

Cleo glanced behind her. The two bloodthirsty hunters were not quite at arm's length, but with advanced yoga training, all bets were off. Fortunately, she had a few tricks of her own— none of which looked as graceful as two barefoot divas, but they were just as effective.

She called this one hustle-and-run. Cleo shoved Tip's other half into the limo, piled in behind, and then slammed the door closed. Sinking down into the plush leather seat, Cleo let out a long sigh of relief. As the limo pulled away, a long list of expletives were hurled at them by the barefooted ladies, though to Cleo's relief they quickly faded to quiet.

As the car turned a corner, Tip's eyes once again started rolling across Cleo from head to toe.

"Creep much?" Cleo snarked at Tip.

"Would you like something to drink?" Tip asked.

"Just water...with lemon. I need to detox with something alkaline. The negative energy in the crowd was insane. It is a dirty job, but someone has to do it," Cleo answered.

"It's like that with a lot of jobs," Tip responded.

Cleo accepted the glass of water from Curtis with a polite nod. Looking back and forth between Tip and his servant, uh, personal assistant, a sarcastic chuckle escaped her lips.

"Sorry..." Cleo shrugged. "...I just don't think our definitions of dirty jobs are the same. But it doesn't matter though. Looks like we made a clean getaway."

"Hmm..." Tip murmured as he slowly eyed her messy ponytail, plain T-shirt, and baggy jeans. "I'm sure someone dressed like you seen jumping into a Maybach went completely under the radar."

"Are you being sarcastic?" Cleo questioned.

"Just like when celebrities rock sunglasses, funny hats, and believe they walk about unnoticed," Tip continued.

"Maybe they do," Cleo countered. "Do you know any celebrities personally?"

"A few," Tip said. "Tracy Mapp?"

"Who's that?"

"He's a running back, but he is really more of a middle linebacker. However, the owner thought he was more of a running back. The problem is he is not particularly good at either position. He is too tall to be a running back and lacking the leadership as well as selfishness to play middle linebacker. What about One and Uno Faith?"

"Can't say I have ever heard of either of them," Cleo answered.

"No, I imagine you haven't. Neither of them is likely to land on any celebrities-behaving-badly lists or have their names in the papers because of paternity lawsuits."

"Papers? Oh! Like TMZ or social media. Okay, okay, okay—I get it. Why? Why are they gay? Trans? Well Trans people can still have "oops" babies too, ya know. So—"

"What?! No! Their names are Uno and One. They are twins—both cornerbacks. The only problem is that they are too short."

"Like the rapper?" Cleo said, as she fought off a smile.

"The what?" Tip took in a deep breath.

As Tip continued, Cleo decided this was as good of a time as ever to show off her rhyming skills. She hadn't thought of *Too Short* lyrics in years. The thought crossed her mind that she should run an experiment. Mutter the lyrics just low enough that Tip would be annoyed but keep talking.

"He's a pimp. The lyrics violate all my feminist principles but also society. Think it allows me to rebel against my rebellion. Revolution against myself. That's deep."

"Oh it's something. As I was saying. They can get the ball, but anyone of average height can out jump them."

"Everybody's got that same old dream.

To have big money and fancy things.

Drive a brand new Benz, keep your bank right here.
Never hear me stutter once because I talk real clear."
Cleo ironically mumbled.

Tip bit and damn near gnawed his lip in determination and continued.

"And they both have the tendency to chase the football groupies—THOTS as the cool kids say—who are way out of their league," Tip explained.

"It's on you, homeboy, whatcha gonna do?
You can take my advice and start workin', fool
Or you can close your ears and run your mouth
And one day, homeboy, ya soon find out.
Life is too short. Too short," Cleo loudly whispered.

Tip nodded as if he was close to figuring out where he had gone wrong in life, if this was what it all had come to after living for 55 years.

"How about Traci Jones? Surely you've heard about her?" Tip questioned while staring out the window.

Cleo's head cocked to the side, curious puppy style. Tip side-eyed Cleo's change from annoying performer to inquisitive ingénue. He smiled like someone that had just won a lottery with a fake ticket. And he moved to cash in the ticket much the same, i.e. before anyone noticed it was counterfeit.

"Finally," Cleo sighed. "Someone who isn't related to football."

"Not exactly," Tip explained. "For the record, I do know non-football related celebrities, but none of them are card carrying PETA members, so I figure they wouldn't interest you."

"Probably not," Cleo agreed. "Alright, I give. Who is she, a cheerleader, football wife, Real Housewife?"

"No, no, and no. Now here's something that might give you that 'I'm a part of something bigger than the football breaking barriers' feeling—Traci Jones is the first female player in the National Football League," Tip said with a cocky grin.

Cleo's eyes widened with shock. "She's a football player?"

Tip chuckled, then said, "I knew that would send your little activist heart aflutter. I'm sure all this name-dropping is boring you. Have you thought about how you are going to pay your restitution?"

"My restitutions?"

"Well..." Tip shrugged, "... you can't just go around dousing mink coat-clad people with red paint and not have to pay for the damages. The world doesn't work that way. Surely, your mother and father told you that."

"My mother and father are dead," Cleo spat defensively.

"Good," Tip thought.

"I'm sorry to hear that," Tip responded.

At that moment, Tip's false sincerity was not of prime concern. Instead, the enormity of her actions and potential consequences were far more worrisome. Sinking further in the seat, Cleo wondered how her perfect play had gone so wrong. Two protests at once. One for social justice and a sneak attack to speak for all the allies of animals. Toss, run, teach those animals killers a lesson. It had worked out perfectly in her mind. She had even made a list of all possible outcomes, but never once had she considered being intercepted by someone like Tip McMann.

"It's summer. Heard them say that there was a sale. She only paid ten grand," Cleo murmured.

Tip's eyes squinted and he made a soft clicking sound with his tongue, as if he was making mental calculations.

"So... rough estimate... you're looking at one hundred hours of community service and two hundred thousand dollars," he said after a brief pause.

"Two hundred thousand!?" Cleo gasped.

"You have to account for emotional damages. Maybe you could refinance your house," Tip offered.

"I'm a renter," Cleo gritted between her teeth.

"I might be able to help you. You have something that I am interested in," Tip said.

"No… just no," Cleo groaned as she scooted further away.

Tip rolled his eyes impatiently. "Someone really thinks highly of herself. You're pretty but not THAT pretty. Actually, I am here to make an offer for your football team."

"My football team? I don't have a football team. I don't even play fantasy football. So I don't even have a pretend team! I don't understand."

"Trust me, at this point, the feeling is entirely mutual," Tip said and then reached for a folder. He pulled out a photograph and handed it to Cleo. "Do you recognize this man?"

Cleo stared blankly at the photograph until memories began to seep from some distant place in her mind. She almost did not recognize him without the pie she had tossed in his face. It seemed like a lifetime ago. Another perfect plan. The only difference was that it had been foiled by his security team.

Tip watched her keenly and saw the recognition on her face. "His name was Walsh Ford. He was the owner of the Detroit Lions. In his infinite wisdom, he felt that the team should belong to you when he passed. Mostly because he hated the NFL and wanted to give them one last gargantuan middle finger before exiting the Earth" he explained.

Cleo grinned like a super villain. Despite her feelings towards Walsh, she admired his style. Tip took notice and frowned.

"Oh, he didn't like you much either and thought the NFL would do just as much to fu-, er… eff you up as you would eff the whole league. In essence, a marriage that would make both of you equally miserable."

"So, what," Cleo laughed with disbelief. "The NFL has turned into the Mega Millions? Where's the oversized check?"

Tip motioned to Curtis and he retrieved a briefcase. "Oversized checks are a thing of the past. We've found that cash is much more convenient," Tip explained, as Curtis popped open the case.

Cleo's mouth was agape. Momentarily speechless, she

finally managed to mutter the first thing that came to mind, "Is that even legal?"

"Rest assured, every single bill in that briefcase was legally obtained. This is the first installment. This is a mere pittance of what you will receive by the end of this week. There is more than enough here to assuage your legal woes and launch whatever altruistic company you envision. Hell, you can start your own animal sanctuary for all those defenseless critters out there. "

As Cleo stared at the cash, Tip's mind began to wander. He was over watching poor people stare at life-changing pieces of paper, be they documents or currency. Even when those pieces of paper could transform his life from rich servant to rich master. An achievement he wanted more than his next breath. His mind wandered to his own *Too Short* limerick

"*You could give a man time but you don't know,*" Tip mumble rapped.

"I'm sorry, what was that?" Cleo asked, without breaking eye contact with the money. Tip smiled and nodded no. Didn't matter as Cleo never looked away from the money. Tip decided to continue his concert changing genres from mumble to whisper rapping.

"In a matter of time, I'll be runnin' the show." Tip muttered.

"Women often shrink when they're bragged about. Be proud of what you've done, and when someone brags about you, acknowledge the credit you've been given. Don't push the credit away."
~ Katie Sowers, Coach San Francisco 49ers

Welcome to this Sunday's Special Edition of Pardon the Interruption, where we focus on three letters, NFL, that stand for "Not For Long", also allegedly known as the National Football League. Well, Tony, it appears you and the people of your ilk who complain about overpaid quarterbacks…

Disney Landover stole a quick glance over her shoulder. Her brown fifteen-year old anime eyes rolled around the living room in the home of Job Lamb, her bestest friend in the world. Well, his father's home, as he was only a few months younger than her. Job was sixteen going on fiddy-two, not fifty-two. When the mood struck him, his demeanor was much like his home, well until whenever Disney blessed it with her presence.

Despite its minimalist museum-like feel, it was more like a series of walls that needed to rotate its collection. Though a visitor, she was a frequent visitor. As such, Disney knew the place better than the residents and could find no distraction in it. And today of all days she needed it: a conversation—more like lecture—she received from her mother was playing on repeat in her mind. She resorted to a loud-ass sigh.

"Sighhhhhhh!" Disney melodically bellowed.

Despite the performance Job was still not paying attention to her, and Disney was used to attention. Whether it was from strangers, friends, family, parents, or acquaintances. Think of a compliment appropriate to give to a 14-year-old girl and Disney had heard it and a few inappropriate ones too.

So many that her mom, Debbie Landover (Disney's twin but 20 years older), didn't just have "The Talk" with Disney. Instead, Debbie had "The Talks" with Disney. Two talks. One for her race and one for her gender. One for the people that would throw shade at Disney because of her shade. And another to warn her about the men, young and old, that would break their promises to her and seek to make her break the promises she made to herself.

Of these two talks, Debbie herself had had the same first conversation with her own mother when she had been Disney's age. But not the second. Well, sort of not the second. Not wanting to make the same mistake as her mother had, Debbie had sat her daughter down just hours ago to talk about men. She hoped to protect Disney from the trauma and the terror that she herself had endured growing up. Hours later, Disney was struggling to make sense of Debbie's warnings. Simply put, Disney, an undiagnosed knowledge hoarder, didn't know what to throw away and what to keep. So much so that her mind now solicited opinions from every other part of her body.

In fact, every Disney molecule was now holding a caucus to agree on which bits to keep and which to allow to fade into subconscious oblivion. Unfortunately, before the voting could conclude, Debbie's words of wisdom were to be played over and over and over again per Robert's, scratch that, Disney's Rules of Order.

"Disney, I've known you for 14 years now. And I can say without a shadow of a doubt, that the only negative thing you may ever hear is, *the problem with Disney is that she knows she's a genius,*" Debbie said with a prideful you-are-my-daughter smile.

KEEP. Disney molecules decided.

"My mom wrote me a song when I was your age, Disney. It had one line. And she repeated it most of my life and hers until, well, I was 30. Except it wasn't a song. It was just something repeated so often it felt like a song. *Don't get pregnant.* It was the verse, chorus, bridge and refrain."

"She had me when she was 14. Yep, your age. She looked just like me. Just like you. If you lined us up, you, me, and her would look like time traveling temporal triplets. She was worried that I would do the same. Maybe this is why the only danger in the world she prepared me for was pregnancy. But she only had 1/3rd of a sex talk with me. Nothing about relating, communication and dynamics of how to relate to people and honing your sense. How to trust your instincts. How to get the sex that you want. Pleasurable wonderful thing. None of that. Don't get pregnant! That was the extent of my mom's sex talk with me," Debbie continued.

RETAIN.

"Trust but verify."

KEEP.

"She never warned me that people would see our celestially ascending high cheekbones, lips that eventually will make someone forget about space and time, chameleon-like colored eyes, that shifted much like our obsidian chiffon skin whose tone deepened most beautifully depending on the angle of light generated by our most important star, and have a reaction that would hurt us. They would see all this and decide to lie when the truth would do to get what they wanted."

DRAMATIC AF, BUT KEEP.

"Oh yeah that little changing eye color thing you got going on is a genetic abnormality called heterochromia. You shouldn't die from it. I mean you won't die from it. I think. Google it. What was I saying? Oh yeah! Your face is best friends with light. Sometimes you don't look real to me. You're not just pretty, Disney. You have a pretty light. A light that shines on every atom of you."

VERIFY.

"Always thought I was kinda smart because people told me that. And I thought I was pretty because people told me that. But you, Disney, you believe those things because *you* told you that."

VERIFY.

"My mom sent me into the world with no other real instructions. No warnings about men and how they use a four-letter word to gain a four-letter word to get what they really want."

KEEP.

"Always let someone know where you are."
BUFFERING.

"Have an escape route."
BUFFERING.

"You are not the guardian of hurt feelings. If the consequence of you saying 'no' is hurting a man's feelings, then so be it."

KEEP.

"You have the right not to kiss, hug, like, or love someone."
KEEP.

"Your mind is pretty. Your way is pretty. Don't think I ever met anyone that actually thinks beautifully. And you're still a child. You're like the Universe, you won't lose your light anytime soon. That might be the most beautiful thing I've ever said. See that! You got all the accoutrements to inspire! All the skills you need to get all the things you want!

"Without saying a word, people will assume wonderful things about you. Things that they want for themselves, for their own purposes. They will want to abuse you or be abused by you. Want to mistreat you or be mistreated by you. Others will want to love you and be loved by you. Some will even want to be hated by you, just as long as you feel something about them."

BUFFERING.

"Remember you have no obligation to any of that. You don't have to be a good girl to be good."

HOLD.

"And when you're ready I'll tell you why I named you Disney."

TABLE.

Just as soon as she thought she had a handle on it, the handle was lost. Her atoms complained that the molecules didn't represent them. The protons followed suit and so did the neutrons until Disney decided to simply ACCEPT all the proclamations. This should have brought relief, but instead brought on more questions.

"Was Job this type of young man that would break his promises to her and make her break promises to herself? Can she trust him?" Disney's heart wondered.

"Could this slim little brown boy with matching brown coco eyes, so practical that he cut his own hair, be her enemy? How could a face like that ever hurt her? A face so sweet and cute that when it was covered in a down-hood trying to survive a Detroit winter, it mistakenly led many a person to tell Job's mom 'your daughter is so pretty'. His mother had to correct them. It was easy to see with those long eyelashes, those lips that looked like symmetrical Tootsie Rolls hanging under a nose, the kind that plastic surgeons would call "The Job". Disney and Job saw eye to eye, both physically and on most stuff. How could anything change that? He looked like an angel. And an angel couldn't break her heart. That's not what angels do," Disney thought as she gently massaged her temples.

Disney's heart continued to think and her mind continued to feel. At least as both pertained to Job. All the while, she stared at Job with a pout that she had perfected with the help of countless selfies. Disney and her curly hair whirled around on the Boca Do Lobo white leather sectional sofa that Job's father had imported from Portugal. She looked out through the twelve-foot high, vaulted, ceiling-to-floor windows at the crystalline blue pool and customized sports court in the backyard below.

The property was surrounded by a small thicket of woods, which gave the illusion of living in isolation, but in reality, several other magnificent estates lay afar. Past those estates was a lake, where many fine memories had been created for the esteemed residents of Bloomfield Hills. Beyond the lake, the driveways grew less pristine and the homes less imposing, and should a person feel adventurous, about thirty miles south, the road eventually led to the famous Motor City itself: Detroit.

Though she looked out through those massive windows onto the property, Disney was unfazed by the stunning view outside. She was much more interested in what wasn't happening inside the house. Had Job ever received "The Talk"? He joked about such things but never seriously discussed it. Had he had someone tell him how smart he was? How his entire being was beautiful? Had the type of things said to him that made him feel confused, weirded out, empowered, special, loved now and forever, like I feel?

"Oh and that's what she was trying to do. Not all of the information applies to the now," Disney thought as her molecules unanimously passed a measure to keep all the Debbisms.

And speaking of the future, back to Job. They could make the perfect couple. Everyone on IG agreed. Whenever she posted a pic with Job, her likes and his likes tripled, though neither cared. But still, it was a fact. Speaking of facts, Job was the only person who appeared unaware of the fact that they made the perfect couple. Once while comment creepin' her post, Job saw that someone had written #ILoveBlackLove. Job wondered aloud, "What does that mean?"

Disney's face wrinkled in a frown. "Uh, what do you think it means? You're Black, I'm Black, and we look like we love each other."

Job's expression grew perplexed. "But ain't you half white tho?"

"N word you know I'm—"

"I feel like your white side is oppressing me right now."

They both burst into laughter. And that was how it always went. Whenever things could get seriously pre-teen romantic, something would happen, always prompted by Job, to lighten the mood. Together, they were like a real-life coming-of-age movie. Today, Disney needed a distraction. In addition to Debbie informing Disney that Disney had an intellectual juggernaut inside her, Debbie had also offered some unsolicited styling advice. Disney turned to distraction once more.

Inwardly grumbling, Disney couldn't believe that she had completed her analysis of "The Talk" only to have her peace of mind give way to the overwhelming desire to dissect the not-so-pleasant exchange of words she had shared with her mother after "The Talk". The whole thing had happened right before she had left for Job's house. Debbie did not want her to wear the strategically torn denim, and the lace trimmed, sleeveless top. Her mom suggested she should save it for the first day of school, but Disney had other ideas. Maybe if Job saw her wearing something other than running shorts and a T-shirt, he might really see her. Maybe if she could stop thinking about anything at all, she thought. The irony of thinking about not thinking pushed Disney too far. She was over herself.

"According to the schedule, our game should have been played thirty minutes ago!" Disney yelled out.

On the other side of the elongated living room, Job sat in one of the customized cinema-style chairs. Disney's one consolation was that he was not only ignoring her, he was also ignoring the ninety-inch LED HGTV that was mounted on the wall in front of him blasting ESPN. His attention was focused on the center table in front of him. In Disney's opinion, that center table was the oddest piece of furniture in the entire house. It was not necessarily out of place with all the other glass-topped, granite, and marble pieces that filled the house, but... it was just weird.

The table was composed of two boxes. One of the boxes

was made from black mirrors, and the other box was out of clear glass. The creepiness factor was inside the transparent box, where two scorpions were permanently transfixed. The docile scorpion lay with his appendages curled into its body. The other, the obvious victor, if the battle had ever been allowed to finish, had both its front claws and tail stretched tall. When Disney and Job argued, disagreed, or debated in this room, Disney often found herself staring at the box wondering which scorpion was her and which was Job.

Disney looked back at the other ninety-inch LED HGTV that was mounted on the wall right in front of her. Yes, there were two TVs in the living room. A Madden game filled the screen to the right just waiting to be played. Just as her annoyance from neglected was a few degrees from hittin' full boil, Disney remembered she was rich... friend-rich. Much like a Hollywood fixer, she had interesting friends in high and low places. Well, more acquaintances rather than friends. Unlike a Hollywood fixer, most of her friends, high and low, were in digital spaces. Disney whipped out her phone so fast, GPS couldn't determine from which of her pockets it came. Hell, it could have come from the cutest little Telfar you've ever seen. Only the fashion gods know.

She grinned as her fingers Milly Rocked across the screen as if IG, Twitter, and Facebook were clubs playing all the jams. Scrolling, liking, commenting, DMing, until her hands were cramping, like each fingertip had been doing all this social dancing in five little fingertip-sized 5" Louboutin So Kate heels. Damn, those shoes are uncomfortable. The pain reminded Disney of the salesperson telling her mom, "These are meant to be worn from the car to the restaurant or the VIP area. Then you sit." Disney shook her head and had one thought as she stretched her hands to squeeze a bit more out of her aching digits, "In five years, I will need to find some comfortable shoes because I refuse to sit my life away in order to rock red bottoms."

At the other end of the room, a familiar rapid-fire Facetime ringtone went laughing through the room. Job hit the accept button on his MacBook like a duck flying south for the winter—out of instinct. But he had little desire to communicate, so much so that he didn't look up from his papers.

Disney's voice echoed. "Boy, you hear me!"

"Yeah… yeah give me a sec. I need to finish paying these bills for my dad. Why don't you figure out my team's strengths and weaknesses?" Job answered as he punched buttons on the calculator.

Disney did not bother to hide her eye roll or the accompanying groan, which had little to do with the fact that he was ignoring her and more to do with the fact that he was once again doing his father's job. They were both still kids for goodness sake.

Job knew exactly where that groan was heading—back to a conversation that he did not want to have… again. Disney was real bright about most stuff, but no matter how many times he tried to explain why things were the way they were, she just could not seem to understand. Before she could call the *complain about Job doing his father's job play*, he would call a distraction. If it worked it's like getting a pick six! They don't say the best offense is a good defense for no reason.

"Push X and go to the Coaching Strategies screen… there. Now scroll over. That's it. Don't you compare teams?" Job asked.

Disney shook her head in denial, so Job asked, "What's your record?" When she did not respond, Job started again, "I said…"

Disney looked over her shoulder with a cocky grin. "Don't worry about that. Worry about your record after I put this whooping on you today."

Job smiled. "It's whoopin' not whooping, unless you plan on spreading some contagious cough. If that's the case, you need to get on out of here."

Disney ignored him and turned her attention back to the screen with a hidden smile. It might not be the kind of attention she wanted, but secretly, it was better than being ignored.

"I'm going to give a whoopin' too," Disney retorted as

the screen flipped unexpectedly. "Hey wait, what did I do? What is this nonsense? I was playing the game, and now I'm stuck in the middle of math class? And why are your Detroit Lion bars higher in every single category: 99 Offense, 99 Defense, 99 Special Teams, 99 overall? What up doe?"

Job's heart smiled when hearing the three words that comprised the quintessential Detroit phrase, used as a greeting but also used sometimes to ask, "What's going on,". The smile would not live long in his heart.

After the owner of the Detroit Lions died, everyone knew that it was only a matter of time before the discussion turned to the future of the team's ancient receiver core, including its tight end Methuselah. At the same time, they have to figure out if their main asset, which came on late in the season to lead them within one game of the playoffs, is worth keeping given that he will be a free agent after this season. Some have...

Job let out a loud sigh and then picked up his phone. A worried frown puckered Disney's lips. *'It was just talk'* she wanted to tell him. 'People talk nonsense all the time. It doesn't mean anything'. But she knew it meant something to Job. If it meant something to Job, then it meant something to her too.

Disney Facetimed Job again. Job let out a sigh as her face replaced the calculator screen on his phone. Disney paced the room as if they were miles apart until she was standing beside him.

"Fine, then I won't say anything else to you. I will just sit over there and work on my team. I won't say anything else because I'm not one of those types that keep talking when someone doesn't want to hear what I have to say," Disney called out.

"You don't say," Job mumbled.

Disney strutted back to her wall-less fortress of solitude.

"Nope, I just shut my mouth because that's what I am: a mouth-shutter. I'm quiet like a monk. You don't have to tell me twice to leave you alone. I'm, like, you just leave me alone and let me do what I have to do. I don't need a bunch of chatter. Just going chit chitty bang bang chitty bang. Just talking and saying nothing. Yep, I..."

A wide smile broke out on Disney's lips when she heard the phone fall to the table and his chair slide back. A few seconds later, Job snatched the controller from Disney's hand and began feverishly hitting buttons. He then motioned for her to scoot over.

"Move child! Let me learn you something about this Madden. See this is your first problem. You have two number one picks and two number two picks. You must have traded some people for those picks… Never do that. Rule number one on Madden is that number one picks are worthless… you know why? DO YOU KNOW WHY?"

Disney flinched and then playfully punched his arm. "No, Preacher Man, I do not know. Why don't you teen boyspain why they are so worthless?"

Disney began to record Job.

"What came first, the chicken or the egg?" asked Job.

"Hmm… the egg."

"The chicken…" Job muttered as he scrolled through the trading screens. "…because actuality precedes potential. So in Madden you pick the chicken, never the egg. I choose the player who I know can perform rather than the player whose performance I can't predict."

Job's mad wizard fingers finally came to a halt. "So let's go to the Trading Block and see who is available. You need a Tight End that is fast and… a better back. You're also gonna want to build your pass rush… you don't have a receiver either. Take these picks and trade them for older players. Second rule of Madden: speed is the most important thing. Repeat after me: 'speed is the most important thing'."

Disney rolled her eyes and repeated in a sing-songish voice, "Speed is the most important thing."

"You can't coach speed," Job reaffirmed. "Trade all your picks for rookies with speed."

"I don't understand," Disney exclaimed impatiently. "Why do I need a fast person on the line? I need strength. I need…"

"Newton's First Law: an object will stay in uniform

motion unless acted upon by an external force," Job explained but when he saw Disney's blank expression, he added, "Why run through someone when you can run around them?"

Job handed the controller back to Disney. "Okay, now you need to play with it for a little while."

"No wait, wait—how do you make them faster in the other categories?"

"Well, see, here, you can't. You have to export the team. You can't just edit a player in the franchise mode. Don't worry about it. You can improve the players in the training camp," Job explained.

When Disney flashed him a guilty smile, Job sighed. "You skipped training camp and the pre-season games. You know that's how you improve players in the game. See look here."

Disney grimaced. "I tried it once, and it was ugly."

Job scrolled back to Pre-Season and started playing. As his player went through the drills and was rewarded more points, his smile grew cockier.

"Now, you take the points and put them here in speed and, let's see... that is a running back—he needs to be able to break the tackle so let's..."

"Woah, hold up. My running back is a woman!" Disney proclaimed with a grin that was confident enough to match his.

"Naw, she's a kicker. She wants to play running back but they won't let her. So she entered the draft as a kicker. Some coder obviously thinks she might make it."

So the question isn't 'if' but 'when' will the Lions trade their sometimes star, sometimes scrub, sometimes sociopath...

Job's hands fell still. Disney glanced over with wide eyes. Job's head dropped low and his eyes slammed shut. They both held their breaths in anticipation.

Shawn Lamb

I think at this point you have to trade him. I know all the stats both on the field and off— including Shawn Lamb's various run-ins with the law...

"It isn't true," Disney vehemently denied.

... in 2014, he was convicted of assault at Neiman Marcus.

Job began to shake his head in frustration. Like a prophet anointed by Khalil Gibran himself, Disney knew where this was going. She paused the TV. Job immediately unpaused. They went back and forth in a pausing-unpausing war. At the same time though, Tony was miles away, delivering his soliloquy from Washington D.C., yet Job was yelling his monologue of defense back at Tony as if he was standing right there in Job's living room. Disney finally surrendered. If Job wanted to eff up the rest of his day and have a pretend argument with reporters, who was she to interfere.

"Yeah but... that wasn't all on him. An elderly woman was shoplifting, and dad was just trying to stop her... maybe a little too aggressively... and he should have had his clothes on... I told him to change in the dressing room, but he wouldn't listen to me... AND a pack of angry shoppers doused him with pepper spray. It's a miracle that he didn't end up in the emergency room."

... and then in 2016, Shawn was charged for another assault in Saks Fifth Avenue...

The controller fell to the ground as Job covered his face and groaned. "Again... when did Mike and Tony turn so biased? They aren't telling the whole story, and they know it. If it wasn't for my dad, who knows how much merchandise would have been stolen that day. Okay sure, maybe Dad shouldn't have taken off his shoe and thrown it across the store to stop the shoplifter, but he's a *football player*. It's his job to throw things."

I know that you are very close to the Lamb family. You helped write Shawn's premature autobiography aptly entitled I'm the Best of All Time *— so defend your boy!*

Since coming into the league in 2010, he has played for Dallas, Atlanta, Baltimore, San Diego, New England, Tampa Bay, Minnesota, and Detroit. He was traded a record three times in one season, but, Tony, I have to tell you he is a character guy. He didn't have trouble until… well, we know. Since coming to Detroit, he has been a model citizen and one of the few bright spots on that team.

But when you compare that to a Tight End such as Methuselah, I mean Landover, who has been with the Lions his entire career and even took less money to stay, you think that there must be something wrong with Lamb if he can't find a home.

Job turned off the television and picked up the controller. Wordlessly, Disney reached for his hand. Job looked up and found big, fat tears in her eyes.

"For EVERY pass I caught in a game, I caught a THOUSAND in practice."
~ Don Hutson, Wide Receiver Green Bay Packers

When Mike Nichols, typical cocky college quarterback, University of Tennessee at Knoxville, to be exact, moseyed over to stand behind Jax Wilson, his 350-pound center, Billie Wall, slammed her whistle between her lips. If there was something Billie could not stand to see on the field, practice or not, it was a mosey. Only a fool believes you get anywhere far in this life with a mosey. Gut instinct, intuition, or maybe the fact that she knew this game and its players better than most of the men that stood on this field, including Mike and Tony, who told her that she was going to make good use of the whistle today.

Mike yelled the count. The ball was snapped. Jeff Anderson, considered an undersized middle linebacker at 215 pounds, charged straight for Mike but was plowed to the ground by Jax. A piercing shrill blasted through the air and all the players froze in motion as Billie strode towards them.

"What was that? What are you thinking about? This is practice! Practice!" she yelled.

Jax's eyes fell to the ground. It was one thing to be chewed out by the coach, Stan Wall, but another thing entirely when his wife was set off. Billie was downright scary and there was not a player on the team who would say any differently—except for to her face. Standing just a pair of five-inch high heels, shy of six and a half feet tall, she stood toe-to-toe with most of the players. A no-frills kind of woman, she considered the fine lines that crossed her face badges of honor. Billie was a stout woman with gorgeous dark brown eyes that so perfectly matched her skin you would think she was genetically engineered. Most players believed she might have the DNA sequence of a Valkyrie. That's if a Valkyrie chose a pixie haircut.

Billie grabbed Jeff by the facemask and pulled him towards her face until they were head to helmet.

"Look at him. Why do you think that you can run him over every play? Do you think Mike Singletary or Junior Seau tried to run over every center they faced …let me answer for you. NO! NO! NO!"

Jeff gulped. He tried to mutter something to defend himself, but before any words came out of his mouth, Billie ripped the helmet off his head and put it on.

"Okay everybody reset," Billie barked.

Billie assumed Jeff's position. She nodded with approval when Mike lined up behind Jax. Nothing like blasting a whistle and a little of Mama's tender, loving fierceness to take the mosey out. Mike once again yelled the count and the ball was snapped. Billie charged towards Mike. Jax prepared to make his block. He extended to push her, but Billie pivoted and pushed him using his weight and momentum against him. Jax crashed to the ground. Billie grabbed Mike's flag.

Billie removed the helmet and walked back towards Jeff. "Now I only have one of those in me per season, but you should have fifty per game. Is that understood?" she asked, as she tossed his helmet back to him.

When he did not immediately answer, Billie yelled, "Is that understood?"

Jeff slammed his helmet into place. "Yes, coach!"

Billie turned around to address the rest of the players, "Okay, set it up and repeat after me... WE PLAY HOW WE PRACTICE!"

In unison the team repeated, "WE PLAY HOW WE PRACTICE!"

"WE PLAY HARD!"

"WE PLAY HARD!" the team recited.

"BECAUSE WE PRACTICE HARD!"

"BECAUSE WE PRACTICE HARD!"

"FUNDAMENTALS FIRST! FUNDAMENTALS FIRST! STRENGTH SECOND!"

Billie glanced over to the side of the field where Stan was being interviewed on *First Take* via remote by Molly Quirem Rose, Stephen A. Smith, and Michael "The Playmaker" Irvin. She wondered if they had caught that. Deciding to see for herself, she announced, "Five-minute break. I will be right back."

"Rumor has it that you are the first man to willingly hire his wife as assistant coach and the only one to win a national title as a result," Molly said.

Stan responded, "Well, Molly, my wife is a consultant, not a coach. I am happy that she is here with me."

"Well, I have tried to get Michael's wife to work here but..." Stephen A interjected with a wide smile.

"What do you have to say about the rumors that your wife is the brains behind your system and it doesn't work without her?" Michael questioned.

Although staying out of the camera shot, a slight smile curled Billie's lips — the first one of the day. Growing up, she had never been like other girls with their fanciful romantic notions of love Romeo and Juliet style. She always knew that if she were ever to get married, she wanted something more akin to Michelle and Barack Obama, two people who worked together to change the world for the better. If Billie and her husband could not change the world, they could at least change the game of football, which was *their* world.

"She is the brains. Without her, I can't find my keys, my phone, or my clean underwear for that matter," Stan retorted.

Billie's smile vanished! She had half a mind to blow her whistle and call a halt to the play.

"I know that you've been mentioned or linked to numerous NFL jobs and everyone agrees that it is just a matter of time. Once that opportunity comes, will your wife be a part of the package deal?" Stephen A asked.

"To be honest, no…" Stan started.

Billie's heart sank like the *Titanic* after it had been wounded by an iceberg and then struck by a torpedo from a nuclear sub. Ripped down the middle, first one half sank to the bottom of the abyss, followed closely behind by the other. But in this scenario, add a mushroom water cloud. So long, Barack and Michelle, instead she was living the White House edition of Hillary and Bill. In a five-minute segment, all her accomplishments and personal sacrifices had been completely negated… by her *husband*. She had given her life to this game, and it came down to this: she was a glorified fetcher of keys and organizer of clean underwear.

"… My wife is wonderful. But she is not a football coach. She is a good consultant and helps the team with things like equipment management and uniforms…"

LIAR… Billie silently screamed.

"…so for any teams that are out there that may be interested in making offers, understand that when it comes to the game of football, we are not attached at the hip," Stan finished.

Stan caught a glimpse of Billie as she walked away with her face buried in an iPad and knew he was in major league trouble.

Seemingly unaware of the tension, Mike continued on, "Finally, do you have any advice for the new owner of the Detroit Lions?"

"Yeah, sell," Stan chuckled. "To the first person stupid enough to buy the headache."

"So it's safe to say that we won't see you coaching in Motown anytime soon," Michael added.

"I wouldn't say that… not at all," Stan denied.

"Okay, thanks for taking the time to be with us. Stan Wall, boys and girls…," Molly finished.

Stan waited until the remote crew left the field before he approached Billie with caution reminiscent of a zookeeper bringing breakfast to a lion at dinner time.

"You've got forty-seconds. Time is ticking. I'm much too busy to stand around dawdling with you. What with the team's uniforms that need pressing, players' lockers that need organizing… and goodness knows, I need to rush home, put on my make-up and heels and make my man a nice hearty dinner because he works so hard while his wife waits around to find his lost keys…"

"*Billie…*"

Billie looked up from her iPad with a glare. "Don't. Don't you even think that you can "Billie" me and everything will be just fine."

"I know you're upset about me saying that you're just a consultant, but I don't want to mess up anything by letting on that they can't have me without you."

Stan reached up and tried to caress Billie's cheek, but she slapped his hand away.

"I know you are important to the team and the system… and I couldn't do any of this without you but… Billie you… this is bigger than us… this is for our family."

Stan stared at Billie like a chef waiting on Michelin to rate their signature dish. Billie returned Stan's pleading gaze with dissatisfaction and more. If looks could kill, she just put Stan on life support.

"But…uh… Billie this is for women everywhere…"

Billie snorted in disbelief. "How? How can you possibly say that now? Just a few minutes ago, you made me sound like your glorified secretary."

"If I can get you on as an assistant, that will be *huge*... but it can't be a situation where everyone thinks you are running the show. No GM wants to risk his job on a husband and wife team. Power perceived is power achieved."

"Power perceived is power achieved," Billie mocked. "How many women do you reckon had to swallow that bulls— platitude while they were waiting in their husband's shadows?"

"We are so close to getting where we want to be, but right now I'm going to need you to man up and get us another championship."

"Why is it only *we off*-camera?" Billie asked and then walked away.

Stan followed. "Did you finish the new plays? I was thinking that we might want to switch to a 4-3 defense against Florida because..."

"Stan, who runs the defense?" Billie interrupted.

Stan pointed at her as they walked towards the team.

"Who runs the offense?"

Once again, Stan pointed in her direction. Billie motioned for the team to begin.

"And what is your job?"

"To coach," Stan answered.

"What is mine?"

"To win games."

"Maybe the next time someone asks, you might want to remember that. Have you spoken to Tip?"

Stan looked away hoping to make that call another time. Tip was a firecracker without filters. You just never knew with Tip. Sometimes his words were dazzling enough to light up a night sky, but other times he uttered nonsense that had the unfortunate consequence of blowing up in other people's faces. Billie had been hounding him to make the call for over a week. Maybe if the day had gone down differently, Stan could have found another excuse to put it off, but as it was, he silently took the phone from her hand and sat down on the bench. Billie bellowed at the players, but Stan knew she would be listening to every word he said.

...

Sitting inside the Detroit Lions owner's box, Tip heard his phone ring. He reached into his pocket with a sneer curling his lips. It was not the ringing that made his mood foul, but instead the idiotic charity cases that were currently cluttering his pristine owner's box. He was all for looking good and giving back to the community so long as the community did not invade his personal space. It wasn't just a personal space issue. It was a safety issue, allegedly.

In Tip's mind, most of the homeless clutter were either alcoholics or drug addicts, otherwise they wouldn't be homeless. Tip chose to conveniently disregard expert reports that less than 40% of homelessness was actually caused by drugs or alcohol abuse. Tip didn't care what the experts thought. Moreover, according to Tip, the number of contagious diseases clustered together in his space was appalling. For goodness sake, the next time someone comes up with the bright idea to invite a bunch of homeless bums to sit in the owner's box, someone needs to at least screen them and pick the ones that do not smell like five-day old Chinese food. It was revolting. At least so thought Tip.

"Tip here. What do you want?"

"Tip, it's Stan Wall."

Tip covered his nose with a tissue and considered asking one of the teams' physicians if they had any extra surgical masks. "Stan, nice interview."

"Yeah, I was hoping you would be able to see it."

"Wouldn't miss it, Stan. Like I said before, I promise you the next job that opens is yours, but no team under my watch is going to put up with what UT did. We are hiring you, not Billie. So that means I will not see her anywhere near that sideline unless she has on black and white stripes with a whistle in her mouth. Is that understood?"

Stan fell silent as he glanced up at his wife.

"Is that understood..." Tip started to repeat his

demand, but as he took a drink from the waiter's tray and at the same time one of the unhoused invitees reached for a glass. He sat the glass back on the tray untouched. Contrary to popular belief, tuberculosis was still prevalent today. The homeless man flashed a smile that revealed several missing teeth. "You know a dentist could probably fix that for you."

"Excuse me?"

"Not you. It will be nothing short of miraculous if I manage to escape typhoid fever or malaria this season... speaking of Billie, she will never be a ten. Heck, my own wife wasn't a ten until I paid a fortune to her plastic surgeon. My point is that she will need a little more flash. If she doesn't want to go under the knife, at the very least you will need to hire a stylist. That's what the fans expect these days and you can blame Facebook and Instagram for that. Filters and apps won't be enough. But we can work out those details later. Right now, it is time for men to be men again so man up... unless you need her... I mean if that is the case then... great," Tip said and then ended the call. Looking around suspiciously, he put his phone in his front pocket for safekeeping.

**CHAPTER
05**

"Don't run too fast through life. You only have one."
~Bo Jackson, Running Back, Los Angeles Raiders

Disney plopped down on the sofa in Shawn Lamb's living room just in time to hear salt-and-pepper haired Al Michaels, the revered *Monday Night Football* co-host, say:

Well, this is the first kick-off for Traci Jones, the first female player in the NFL, hailing from Tennessee…

Disney leaned forward towards the screen, resting her elbows on her knees. Her feet tapped in a mad rhythm against the plush carpet as she wondered what Job could possibly be doing that was more important than this. "The game is about to start!"

A lot of good players have come out of that school, and I hope that Traci can live up to the tradition… John Madden added while running his hand through his white hair.

A few moments later, Job emerged from the kitchen with two bowls in his hands. He handed one bowl to Disney. "Okay, pour the caramel slowly as I stir."

"Why don't we just put the…" she started to suggest but was cut short.

"Because I don't want to get the caramel on the table."

"Well, then if you…"

Job groaned. "Just pour it."

Disney rolled her eyes as she poured the caramel. "For goodness sake, you are acting like we are in chemistry class or something. This is easy..."

"Ouch," Job winced before she could finish, as hot caramel dripped onto the back of his hand. Despite the pain, his grip on the bowl remained firm.

"Sorry. I don't understand why you can't just buy caramel corn like normal people. You're so persnickety."

"Ouch!" Job cried out again as more hot caramel dripped on his arm. "Get a towel. Get a towel now… the caramel is burning my hand… don't want to drop the caramel corn!"

"You're greedy, greedy," Disney called out on her way to the kitchen.

"Yes, I know! Just get a *towel*!"

Disney returned with a cold wet towel and gently wiped Job's hand clean. Once the crisis was averted, they sat down on the couch together and started eating the caramel corn. Between sticky bites, she grumbled, "You're greedy for real."

Despite the ooey gooey Job's teeth managed to remain pearly white when he flashed a mischievous smile. Disney laid her head on his shoulder, trying very hard to forget that they might not have many more times together like this. She was one of the lucky ones. Not many football brats got to stay at the same school. Some of them, like Job, got shuffled to a new city nearly every season. Disney had seen more than a few come and go, which was the reason she had been hesitant when he first moved to town. Distance shouldn't matter with Facetime, but it does. Within a few months, you just sort of forget about each other. The thought brought tears to her eyes.

Job must have been thinking the same thing. He expelled a quiet sigh. "I'm going to miss you."

Disney wondered how he did that. He could read her mind and take the words straight from her heart. She sat tall and reached for his hand. "He's not traded yet. We better get some

Neosporin on your hand. It looks like it is starting to blister."

"I said *ouch* for good reason. Dad keeps all his medicines in the cabinet above the sink."

"I'm surprised your dad hasn't started with the homeopathic stuff yet. Or maybe that's my mom. They keep aloe plants at the house for burns and essential oils for all the other stuff."

Disney walked back into the living room with a tube of Neosporin in hand just in time to hear Michaels—

With all the rumors surrounding this team, you gotta wonder if Shawn Lamb is going to be more than a little nervous today even though this is pre-season.

Madden responded:

When I coached, the pre-season wasn't part of the season and still isn't. I mean it's rare that a quarterback and team will be judged harshly in pre-season, but with an owner who, from what it says here, was given the team a few hours ago, the first female player, a shaky secondary, and quarterback, who claims that he is alone in couples' therapy because he has fallen out of love with football! This game could define the future of this team. I expect that Lamb will probably be nervous, but as the game goes, he will settle in.

...

Traci Jones took a deep breath. With clenched fists, she gazed up at the crowd. She had dreamed of this very moment for many years, both in sleep and while wake. This was *her moment...* yet it was nothing at all like she thought it would be. She should be hearing the crowd roar her name, but instead all she heard was her heart pounding in her chest, so hard that it felt like it was drumming in her throat.

Don't fuck up... don't fuck up... don't fuck up... the words rang in rhythm inside her mind. Taking one last breath, she ran towards the ball. As soon as her foot made contact with the football, the drumming and chanting fell silent and she felt it... felt it somewhere deep in her soul. *This was her moment.* It was a perfect kick. Time itself seemed to slow down as she watched the ball sail with a faultless arch towards the goal post... then... then it began to curve.

No!

Then... at the last second, the ball went out of bounds and the referee threw a flag.

Illegal procedure on kicking team, forty-yard penalty, FIRST DOWN... the referee announced.

Traci ran to the sideline. Ripping off her helmet, she ignored all the men surrounding her, including the coach. The team gave her a moment until eventually Tracy and Shawn ambled towards Traci.

Shawn side-eyed Tracy with a "Y" as they approached Traci with an "I" and the similarity of names between the two made Shawn chuckle. The humor was lost when the side-eye transformed into a look. A real look, a seeing, where for some reason Shawn began to compare himself to Tracy. Why, he wondered. That's until he realized the 'why' was unnecessary. The look was fully funded by some emotion he did not understand. An emotion that did not need a 'why' to justify its existence. Simply stated, it was what it was, even if he wasn't quite sure what it was. Maybe going through with the comparison would help him figure it out.

Looking at Tracy was like looking at a mirror. Sort of. Sure Tracy had a stout running back's build while Shawn was built like a linebacker that for some reason could toss the football with such accuracy that his arm might be mistaken for an SR-1 marksman rifle. Tracy and Shawn would never be mistaken for one another.

Shawn wore a fade that faded into a small fro depending on his mood. While Tracy was bald by choice. Tracy also had no facial hair except for a five o'clock shadow that he nursed into a full beard in the off season. Both Shawn and Tracy commanded attention. Each was listed at 6'4 though clearly he was two inches taller than Tracy.

Tracy probably, like many athletes, when it came to height, lied in high school, lied in college, and stuck with it. If it ain't broke, don't fix it. Shawn remembered his coach telling him to fudge a bit and tell recruiters he was 6'5. Problem with lying was once you started, it was difficult to stop. Why lie when the truth would do? He was just as proud to be 6'4 as he was of his onyx skin. Just as proud of his 220 pounds as he was of his aging chiseled frame.

Tracy once teased Shawn about a semblance of a love handle. Shawn used his long piano fingers to trace his full lips before telling Tracy, "You'd better hope when you are old enough to have any semblance of a love handle that you have a spot in some team's locker room and a rookie who can tease you before a game."

Tracy stared back at Shawn's true lying eyes. True because when Shawn spoke, his pupils narrowed in such a way that you felt like he was telling you the God's honest truth no matter how much that truth hurt. Lying eyes because Shawn's eyes looked so dark you thought he was wearing contacts.

Shawn told everyone that his eyes were black despite many optometrists letting him know that possessing black eyes, true black eyes, was as possible as Shawn blinking faster than the speed of light. His peepers had enough melanin to reach the darkest brown of browns, a few shades lighter than true black. But like Tracy and two inches, Shawn didn't let two shades of fact get in the way of a good story. Nor did Shawn's fans, wooed by his confidence saying his eyes were black and referring to himself as Night.

Something about Tracy was so familiar, it felt like a reflection. Just as the answer was about to come to him, they sat down on either side of Traci. As they did, Shawn's desire to compare was supplanted with a desire he hadn't felt in so long he thought he was feeling it for the first time.

"Gotta do better," Tracy said as he nudged her shoulder with his.

Traci stared straight ahead ignoring both of them. Her

lips were clamped tight because she was afraid if she opened them even the tiniest bit, tears would escape her eyes. As it was, she had to keep her eyes opened unnaturally wide to keep those stupid little traitors from slipping down her cheeks.

"Are you getting ready to cry? There's no crying in football," Tracy said with a chuckle.

And there it was. In that moment, Shawn realized why Tracy was so familiar. Tracy wasn't Shawn's mirror. He was a window. A window that revealed a ghost-like reflection of a Shawn that lacked all the wisdom accumulated many cell divisions ago. Odd way to count time but it helped him to ignore the many skyscrapers full of bad decisions as he imagined himself looking out the window over a city made up of his past.

In reality, it made for a dope picture. He reflected over the city like a God distracting himself from the truth... what a jerk he was. He was once a jerk that in moments of need would be even less supportive than Tracy. Shawn would wonder as to why Traci accepted that behavior, but that had as much point as asking why her fiancé behaved that way. He already knew why. She loved Tracy almost as much as Tracy loved Tracy. A little fact he would keep to himself. At this point, Shawn only wanted the type of problems that duct tape could solve. Besides, who was he to tell the truth and ruin a great couple hashtag like #TraciTracy.

"Bullshit," Traci grunted. She had spent enough time on fields and locker rooms to know that football players could be some of the whiniest bunch of babies in this crib known as the world.

Tracy shook his head, threw up his hand and popped to his feet like someone waiting for a caller to yell out their number at bingo.

Shawn leaned forward until she was forced to meet his eyes. "Traci, you got a lot of people depending on you. There are little—"

Traci interrupted without turning to look at Shawn.

"...girls watching this game with their mothers and

fathers for that matter... for the first time."

"And there are old and young men and even some women out there that want you to fail!"

"Do you think I don't know that?" Traci spat. "I know exactly what is at stake. And I know that they just watched me choke." She stared at the 45-yard line as her teammates took the field defensively disadvantaged because she had made an illegal kick.

Shawn laid his hand on Traci's shoulder pad. Traci's eyes met Shawn's. Despite all the stadium noise, Traci could hear one thing, her heart beat once, then twice, and then four times.

"If you let me finish, I was going to say that for now, you only need to worry about your 32 teammates who themselves make mistakes everyday so they empathize with you and are too busy worried about their own jobs to be mad because you made one bad kick," Shawn said matter-of-factly.

Traci subtly nodded in concurrence.

"You tried to make the right football play! It didn't work out this time. But that kick is gone, so forget about it, and concentrate on the next one. Now you can cry, but you gotta keep playing. So play and cry. And forget about what *this* guy just told you. There is crying in football cause football hurts like a mutha." He gestured towards Tracy. "You won't be the first player crying on the field and you won't be the last one either," Shawn finished.

Begrudgingly, a slight smile began to tickle her lips. Traci stood up and placed her hand on Shawn's shoulder and counted her skipping heartbeats... one, three, five, seven. Traci removed her hand.

"Thanks," she mumbled, walked towards the practice kicking area, and wiped her tears.

…

Is this baseball or football? Madden asked.

Job's hands covered his face. Even though he didn't

want to, he peeked between the cracks of his fingers.

"I don't know, John." Job said, as if he was at the game rather than in his living room.

Equally dismayed, Disney cried out, "Why are the defensive backs playing so close?"

"Because Dallas is about to score."

They watched in silence as the wide receiver caught the ball. He stopped at the goal line. With his hands wrapped around the ball, his feet wobbled and crossed the line.

Job jumped to his feet. "Oh come on!"

Talk about an unselfish play. That's good football there… Madden chuckled.

Yeah, if you're a Cowboy fan… Michaels answered.

The camera momentarily panned to Shawn. Job watched as his father put on his helmet. The camera returned to the field. He grimaced as Dallas kicked for the extra point.

"Come on, Dad. You've got this," Job whispered.

'Dad?' Disney said to herself, as if Job had whispered he wanted grass for dinner.

Disney, in all the years she had known Job, had never heard him call his father, father, dad, daddy, papa or anything close to something that represented his paternal place in Job's life. Whatever was happening today was something with greater stakes than a football game. As Disney sat next to Job she noticed his hands were clenched tighter than an MMA fighter executing a chokehold. As her eyes walked up his arms to his shoulder, she saw in his sunrise eyes tears welling up. As her eyes walked back down his arm at least one of his fists unclenched and he grabbed her hand. An already weird day had just gotten weirder. As their hand embrace grew delightfully tighter, Disney was left with a three-letter thought… WTF.

"There is no primer for being an NFL owner. It is learn-as-you-go."
~Jimmy Haslam, Owner, Cleveland Browns

"Shawn!!" As with most other things they did, One and Uno, the twins and their huge frames, shouted Shawn's name in unison as he readied himself to take the field.

Shawn seemed to almost skip over with a confident swagger. "I got this." He patted them both on the head and then dashed across the field.

Inside the huddle, Shawn tapped his helmet and then shook his head from left to right. Shawn's eyes whirled back towards the coach and discovered he was shaking his hand at him.

Bristling with mettle, Shawn clapped his hands together. "Okay, Tracy, we are going I-form HB smash. Wideout, I need you to sell this."

Tracy's head waved in opposition. "Nah, I'm not going up the middle till after halftime. Pitch right."

Rolando Brock, a massive center, stood tall. "Look, the play is up the middle, not to the right. Ain't no time to be scared… now if you scared, go to church… this is football Sunday and we need to get the run established. If you go to the right side, that middle linebacker kills you because Branson ain't fast enough to pick him up."

Branson Landover, All-Pro tight end, 6'5, 255 pounds. Trying to tackle him was like trying to chop down a redwood with a plastic butter knife. Well, unless your name was Disney Landover, as Branson seemed to grow weak whenever his daughter asked him for anything. Often when faced with the prospect of saying something that was bound to make someone less than happy, Branson would say to himself, "Well, at least Disney loves me," which gave him the confidence to proceed with the unadulterated truth.

"There is a very high likelihood that I'm not fast enough to accomplish the task necessary for Tracy's plan to succeed."

Rolando and Tracy looked at each other and then back at Branson.

"Tracy you are going to get your ass tore out the frame," Branson said like an untipped fortune teller.

Tracy's eyes flashed with defiance. "I'm going right."

Rolando's head bobbed back-and-forth between Shawn and Tracy as if he were watching a tennis match. "It ain't your call. Shawn, which way we going?"

Everyone looked at Shawn. As he felt their eyes burning into his skull, the words he intended to speak became lodged in his throat. What sort of crazy nonsense was this? Tracy knew Shawn was the captain and as such made the call. The huddle was neither the time nor place to commit mutiny.

Tracy stood tall and took a step back. "Right it is."

The huddle disbanded. From the corner of his eye, Shawn saw Rolando shake his head with disgust. As the team assumed their positions, Shawn realized that he could not wait until the next practice to address this insurrection. The ball was snapped. Shawn pitched right. Tracy ran to the left but then countered to the right. The entire defense took the bait and went left, except the middle linebacker.

Tracy saw the player move past the blocking attempts of the O Line like a lawnmower moving through blades of grass and charging his way. He tried to dodge the middle linebacker, but those pesky laws of physics just wouldn't bend. His momentum pulled him like a magnet. A second later, Tracy was lying immobile on the ground and the middle linebacker was in the end zone displaying his dancing skills for the crowd.

Sitting inside the owner's box, Cleo rested her elbows on her knees and covered her mouth with her hands. Befuddled… completely, and utterly befuddled is the only word that came to mind to describe what she was feeling on the inside. Ever since she found out she owned a team, she had dedicated her life to learning all she could about football.

Admittedly, it had only been a few hours since Cleo had been informed of her new asset but still… she had tried. Cleo swallowed multiple chuckles that almost escaped her lips as she attempted to convince herself that she had somehow learned enough during the car ride to render an opinion. Simply put, Cleo did not know shit from Shinola when it came to football, but she knew a train wreck when she saw one… and this train wreck now belonged to her.

Cleo gasped as she ran her fingers through her hair. "What is he doing now?" Her finger was pointing towards what appeared to be the coach as he ran across the field. Though she could not make out his face, even from her distant vantage point, his animated movements made it obvious that he was having a come-to-Jesus moment with the team's quarterback, Shawn Lamb. The big screen blared in the background like a Greek chorus.

Al, what quarter is it?

I believe it's the first but it appears that it may be halftime… at least in the coach's mind… Michaels answered.

"What now?" Cleo groaned. "Where is he going? Can someone please tell me where he's going?" she demanded, as the coach left the field. Though the suite was filled with team executives and the usual owner box suspects, all were quieter than airplane hostages.

Tip smirked like a tarot card reader that just won the lotto. He nonchalantly leaned forward in his seat. "Oh, I think the coach just quit."

Cleo stared back at him with disbelief. Surely, that could not be true. People didn't just up and quit. Okay... maybe she *had* walked out of a few jobs, but they were the kind that paid minimum wage. She wasn't pulling down seven figures, and she certainly was not coaching an NFL team. Besides, even if it was true, how could he possibly remain so calm? "Quit?"

"You know... Stan Wall could turn this team around."

Cleo flashed him a doubtful expression. "I don't think an act of God could turn this team around."

"Hmm..." Tip muttered. "You know, Cleo... football isn't a game for people with little faith. At this point, you have to be asking yourself, why bother? If you aren't, I know I am asking for you. Your talents... your passions, do you really want to waste them on this?"

Cleo's eyes narrowed with suspicion. "What about your wasted talents and passions?"

Tip sat back in his seat. "I'm too far gone. I'm that old dog that can't learn any more tricks."

Cleo wondered if he seriously believed she was that naive. She had been upfront and honest about her lack of football knowledge, but at least she knew a player when she saw one. "I don't believe you."

"It's true," Tip chuckled. "Trust me; I don't want to see it end like this... with kickers that can't kick, coaches that can't coach, and players that can't play. It's a travesty! The best I can hope for is for someone to right this ship, so my legacy doesn't sink to the bottom of the ocean. But you, Cleo, you don't need this. You're young, you have your whole life ahead of you, a chance to do something bigger than football. Right now, you could get top dollar for the team if you sell."

I'm not sure about the order of succession. I have to check the constitution, but I think after the offensive coordinator, then the GM and VP of Publicity... Madden said.

While Detroit's offense started taking the field, Rolando grabbed Shawn's shoulder. "Shawn, it's on you. The coaches are gone."

Shawn stifled his groan as the team huddled. He already knew that. He also knew that none of this would have happened if Tracy had just accepted his call for the I-form HB smash instead of going right.

Before Shawn could speak, Tracy leaned forward. "Okay, hit me in the flat...no I'm going to run a flat then fly."

Shawn stood tall with his arms spread wide in frustration. This wasn't a backyard game of football. Was Tracy having some sort of identity crisis? First, he thought he was captain and now he's a wide out.

Mimicking Shawn's thoughts, Branson Strong, a 6'3 all muscle cross between a gazelle and Godzilla and the closest thing to a star wideout the Lions had, calmly responded, "You're a running back not a wide out. Shawn, what play should we run?"

Shawn tried to gather his thoughts, which felt as scattered as a ten-thousand piece puzzle in the sticky hands of a two-year-old. He wondered if he had taken one too many hits or maybe just lost his nerve. "We need to try... something different... like using the pass... a short..."

Tracy clapped his hands. "See, I need to run out the flat and shoot towards the end zone. BREAK."

With all the players looking towards him, Shawn just nodded because he could not think of anything else to say. The huddle broke and the team set. Shawn scanned the defense, then yelled, "Blue 42, Cadillac, hut, Red 18, Omaha hike!"

Rolando snapped the ball. Tracy ran to the flat then shot full speed up field. He passed the DB. Tracy waved his hand for the ball. Shawn launched a missile and Tracy caught it, made a football move and... well, Tracy fumbled and fell down. The DB picked up the ball as easily as someone choosing fruit off the shelf at Whole Foods. Shawn rushed to attempt a tackle. Suddenly, a linebacker knocked Shawn off his feet. Shawn lay on the ground, as the DB high steeped into the endzone like a drum major from Tennessee State.

A few moments later, Tracy stood over Shawn. Shawn held his hand up, but instead of reaching for it, Tracy squatted down beside him.

"You hung the ball up there wayyyy too long. Then you don't even tackle him. Man, you're our last line of defense," Tracy said, as if they were having a conversation over kombucha.

...

Sitting together on the couch, Job and Disney watched the game together until the bitter end.

And the final score is Detroit 3, Dallas 42. John, have you ever seen an offense that ineffective?

No, it was like watching a high-school team play a college team. Shawn Lamb threw more interceptions than receptions. In fact, I think he just threw another.

I'm pretty sure he didn't since the game is over.

I don't know, Al, after that performance he may be throwing them from the team bus and then a few more from the airplane.

> *"Most important thought, if you love someone, tell him or her, for you never know what tomorrow may have in store."*
> **~Walter Payton, Running Back Chicago Bears**

Thank you, Creator, for all the blessings that you have bestowed upon me today. I… need a favor… I take that back… just let everything work out for the best and according to your will. Peace be unto me.

Job slowly stood and started walking back towards his bed. Halfway across the room, he abruptly spun around on his heels, ran back to the balcony, and once again dropped down to his knees.

I'm sorry, but I know what I want… I want to stay here with Disney and my dad in Detroit. I want my dad not to be traded. Please help me, help us! I don't care about the consequences, please! That's all I want… nothing more… I just want to be with Disney! Peace be unto me.

Job's eyes fluttered open. He felt a slight tremble cross his lips. Perhaps it was a side effect of silently mouthing — groveling, begging the powers that be. Yet, instead of feeling humbled, he felt the tight clench that wrapped his heart with fear lessen ever so softly.

Job looked at the letter on his bedside table that he had hastily scrawled after Disney had left. They were not kind words, but they were true—in that moment. He considered his original intention of allowing Shawn to find the letter, but reconsidered.

Instead, Job opened the envelope, tucked the letter under his pillow, and left the money on the table. A smile crossed his face as he adjusted his pillow. He knew that any minute now, Shawn would come to his room under the guise of checking on him, but they both knew the real reason was that he was looking to make sure Job paid all the bills. As odd as it may seem to the outside observer, á la Disney, for a 16-year-old to run his father's finances, the alternative was far more anomalous. Unbeknownst to Disney or anyone, save for this father-and-son duo of Job and Shawn, it was a compromise de rigueur, the least one could do.

A league saving trade if you will, executed moments before the trading deadline and seconds before Job's heart relocated to a zip code forever off-limits to Shawn. Franchise for forgiveness. For Job, controlling the money was an act of mercy, an allocation of grief that exceeded the salary cap of pain any one person should bear, especially a child. It was all he could bear after his father had made him a motherless child. Game management for grace. It made him feel closer to her to assume her duties. It made him feel like he became his own father and mother in her death. It made Job feel in control.

For once in a very long time, Job did not worry about his father. No, instead, his mind filled with thoughts of an angel. She was the most beautiful woman Job had ever known. Her Sahara midnight sky skin shimmered like she was dipped in stars. She had a statuesque physique. Whether in calm and peace or storm and fury, she always spoke, moved, and acted with a graceful, regal bearing. She was Day Lamb—his mother.

It was only in moments like this, drifting somewhere between sleep and wakefulness, that he could remember her voice with absolute clarity.

I know you're tired. I know you're worried. But today is your day. The day that you find out what type of man… what kind of person you want to be… Now, you can be the type who says okay I gave a good show and people think that I'm good… or you can be the person who truly expects the best of themself… that says, "I compete against me and outdo myself." You can be the king of you today. So what's it going to be? What are you?

"The king of me, Mama," Job muttered just before he fell asleep.

"If you live long enough, lots of nice things happen."
~George Halas, Player, Head Coach, Owner Chicago Bears

The next day Job and Shawn headed out for a little retail therapy. Neither of them mentioned the disastrous game or what the future might hold. There were a lot of things Job and his father did not talk about — things they probably should talk about but just didn't. Instead, they filled the silence with football conversations when it was a safe subject, and nonsense when it wasn't.

Job could not remember the last time his father had asked him about anything important, such as school and the like. In fact, Job had quit showing Shawn his report cards after elementary school. He guessed there were only so many times a man could look at his son's straight-As and pretend to be impressed. Besides, school was always a sensitive subject. Job only had to mention what was served in the cafeteria before Shawn came home the next day with a new iPhone, or the newest widescreen curved HDTV, Super MacBook... what not. It was guilt —the guilt of having dragged his child to more schools than most military brats, the guilt of trying to play the roles of two parents and failing at both, the guilt of knowing that playing the game he loved was slowly damaging his body in ways that possibly could never be healed.

Yet, they never talked about any of those things. Today, for once, Job was glad about it. He woke this morning with the half-sleep memory of his Mama fresh in his head. Even from heaven, she had found a way to comfort him and renew his strength and determination. True kings don't kick another man when he is down. No, they rise to the occasion ready to face any battle that might lie ahead.

Job figured to play a part, is to dress a part, is to be the part. Shawn wanted to go to Footaction, so Job decided he would buy a pair of the latest LeBron Colorways. While he was at it, he might purchase a few Loro Piana V-necks and a Louis Vuitton belt. It was time to be a king.

As soon as they entered Footaction, Shawn was accosted by fans wanting him to sign their jerseys. It was just the sort of thing he loved, but Job not so much. One thing about his dad, he always handled it like a pro. From the armchair professionals, who wanted to give him their sage advice, or vultures, who saw him as a walking-talking ATM machine, Shawn could handle them all with a charming smile on his face.

Instead of standing around watching Mr. Football handle the crowd, Job decided to browse the inventory. Although he had already made up his mind about the LeBron's, he wasn't above looking for a solid secondary.

Around the Horn was playing on the overhead monitors throughout the store. Tony Reali was moderating a debate between some journalist Job didn't know and Kimberly A. Martin. Job glanced up at the monitor to hear him say, *Kimberly, my dear, dear friend, Shawn Lamb is a very nice guy. Very athletic! He has natural skills although he can't throw well from the pocket. I met him and his son, but it is clearly time for him to go. A move will allow them to…*

Tony muted the anonymous journalist, but not nearly soon enough for Job's taste. Athletic? Natural skills? Can't throw from the pocket? All false coded language used to describe a Black quarterback. Was it too much to ask for just one day… one day…

just one where he didn't have to hear his father being discussed by an old white sports reporter, who couldn't understand what it meant to play the game of football as a Black quarterback in a league where historical Black quarterbacks were not treated like white quarterbacks, i.e. fairly?

Job's heart wandered to Joe Gilliam, the first Black quarterback to start week one in 1974. "Jefferson Street" Joe Gilliam, named after the popular avenue by his college alma mater Tennessee State University, lost his starting job with the Steelers to Terry Bradshaw, despite having a 4-1 record at the time. Terry, who would go on to win a Super Bowl that year as well as a few more and end up as a highly paid broadcaster. Meanwhile Joe suffered from drug abuse problems, was eventually arrested for attempting to rob a fried chicken restaurant with a butter knife, and died at 49.

The reason why Joe was set on this path and Terry on his path... Was it the fact that Joe had a winning record at the time of his benching? Or was it, as Terry suggested, that the community of Pittsburgh and the NFL in 1974 were not too comfortable with an African-American at quarterback? And has anything really changed? Well, let's see: in 2018, one Texas Superintendent took to Facebook after his favorite team lost and wrote,

"That may have been the most inept quarterback decision I've seen in the NFL," he wrote. "When you need precision decision-making, you can't count on a black quarterback."

According to researchers on the topic, the best compliments a Black quarterback will receive are about his physical abilities, something like: "great footwork" or "boy is he fast". Skills related to a quarterback's intelligence—"he sure can read a defense" or "what an example of leadership"—those are saved for the white players.

Patrick Ferrucci, a journalism professor at the University of Colorado, published a study in 2017 that found that most white college students rated Black quarterbacks as less intelligent than white ones, even when the Black quarterback was identified as highly intelligent.

"There are so many studies that prove it; every single published piece of research finds the exact same thing," said Ferrucci in an interview about his work for Global Sport Matters, "It's always a brain versus brawn dichotomy."

So today of all days Job was not interested in hearing the comments of someone that would never care to understand what it was like to live life as a Black man on or off the field.

Tony's voice sounded from the monitor. *The question is whether this is a good thing for Shawn, not the Lions, Kimberly?*

Kimberly answered—*It's definitely a good move for Lamb because now he can go to a team that has more viable weapons, an experienced owner, and a coach. No one wants to play for a team whose coach walks off the field leaving the mascot in charge.*

True as it may be, Job shook his head with disgust and bolted out of the store. He could get everything he wanted online and not have to be subjected to a bunch of strangers calculating the best moves for his future.

Leaving Shawn to bask in glory, Job walked aimlessly. He thought back to the dream he had had of his mother the night before. And how something in that moment had felt like an actual answer to his prayers. But then, doubts began to creep inside his mind. *So what if he had a dream of her? He had dreamed of her before. And so far, nothing had changed.* Like a broken record, every other season brought a new city and new strangers he called friends. The only certainty was that none of them would be Disney.

Lost in dismal thoughts, Job suddenly felt something tug on his pant leg. He looked down and saw a middle-aged, scruffy homeless man sitting on the ground holding an empty cup towards him.

Job blinked with surprise and reached into his jeans pocket. He felt ashamed. The world was filled with people who had to live like this, and here he was bemoaning a future, which would, no doubt, include living in another two million-dollar estate.

Job pulled a five dollar bill out of his pocket and placed it in the man's cup. He noticed the man was wearing a GameStop uniform. It was tattered and dirty, but Job had seen enough of them over the years to recognize it. He even still wore the name tag, *Eli*. "They aren't paying you enough these days."

"Aww…" Eli waved. "Tough times but better days are coming. Of that I'm sure." He spoke with the gentle assuredness of one of those monks from the St. Bonaventure monastery in east Detroit. Straight outta of the D maybe, but a monk Eli was not.

Job folded his arms over his chest as he silently pondered whether or not Eli's illogical sense of optimism was chemically induced. "How? How can you be so sure? No offense, but it seems to me your situation doesn't look so bright and sunny."

"That's cause you got your head up in the clouds where the air is too thin, son. Sit with me for a spell," Eli answered, as he patted the ground beside him.

"I've… you know I would… but I've got things to do."

"Oh…" Eli moaned. "Don't you know, your troubles will be right there waiting for you when you return? They don't mind none if you shake loose for a time."

Job crouched down so they were on the same level and immediately noticed Eli's piercing eyes. Much too bright and sharp for someone who was not all the way there. This made him feel even worse about himself, for having made such quick assumptions about a homeless person. "My troubles?"

"You've the look of a troubled soul if ever I saw one."

Job shook his head with disbelief as he fell back onto his seat. "Troubled soul? I'm too young to have a troubled soul."

"Well… I was just thinking the same thing myself, but it didn't seem proper to make mention."

Job laughed at the strange man. "Where are you from? You don't sound like you are from around here," Job said. Eli did not sound like a Detroit native or even like someone from this century.

"I'm a traveler, you could say. Much like you."

"So..." Job shrugged his shoulders "...you're some sort of GameStop vagabond?"

Eli began rummaging through his bags. "Something of that nature, and I suspect amongst my wares we might find something to your delight."

Job started to stand. "Thanks but no thanks."

"Right...here," Eli exclaimed as he pulled out a Xbox x PlayStation box.

Job eyed the box wearily and was about to leave when he noticed something odd. "Wait, what type of PlayStation is this? It doesn't even have a number? When did they do a collab?"

"You see...," Eli started to explain as he handed the box to Job for a closer inspection, "...this is a prototype. It's special... magical, you might say. It plays all the games and remixes them... adds new features," he finished with a DJ impression.

Job opened the box and discovered a chrome edition. It wasn't like anything he had ever seen before. "How much?"

"Nothin! But, now look, once it's yours, it's yours. Ain't no trade backs. I mean when you get what you ask for, that's it. I'll take twenty for it."

"Twenty, huh?" Job grunted as he reached into his pocket again. "How do I know it works?"

"Just like football... just like life... you don't know if it works until it works. But in the end when it does winning solves all your problems, right?" Eli answered, his wise eyes looking deeply into Job's as he gave him a slow nod of assurance. *Why'd he mention football? Coincidence. I'm too young to believe in coincidence. This is like the beginning of a scary movie.* Job stared deep into Eli's eyes and gave a nod of nervous agreement.

"We would ACCOMPLISH many more things if we did not think of them as IMPOSSIBLE."
~Vince Lombardi, Head Coach Green Bay Packers

The next Sunday Job and Disney were once again camped out in Job's living room watching the game. Today the Lions faced the Ravens. Throughout the week, Job had had a good feeling about this week's matchup, but the positive vibes slowly diminished as the Lions held their score of seven steady while the Ravens rocket-blasted to forty-two.

Job reached for the remote. "I can't watch this."

"Don't give up yet," Disney chided. "You promised all week that this was the game, and the game ain't over yet."

Job stood up and walked across the room. "You go on. I've got better things to do than watch another smack down. In fact…"

Disney leaned forward as the sparkle of something shiny caught her attention. "What is that?" Scooting off the couch, she joined him across the room where he was hooking up a PlayStation that made Disney's hands jet out like a wideout trying to catch a Hail Mary. "When did you get this? It's NICEEEEEEE," she murmured, as she reached down to stroke the chrome.

Job playfully pushed her hand away. "Hey, no

smudges… yet."

"Next generation, PlayStation x Xbox? Have you played it yet?" she asked, as she whipped out her phone with the quickness.

"Nope, I was waiting for you. Oh and I'm not said Playstation x Xbox. It's too many words. This a Playstation!"

"Hmmm, I don't see any rumors of a new PlayStation," she said, without looking up from her phone.

Once Job finished hooking up the PlayStation, he inserted Madden. A blinding flash glowed from the screen, and they both recoiled, covering their eyes.

"Woah…" Disney exclaimed. "What was that? Is this some sort of AR?"

"I don't think so," Job answered, as the menus flashed on the screen. Job frowned and shook his head as he noticed that all the players were listed—even the most recent trades and free agents. Job's confused look often confused itself with his angry look. "This doesn't make any sense. It has all the information, even the trades that happened last week…I don't understand."

"Is that a new copy of Madden?"

"No, same game," Job muttered, as he located the trading block screen and found that Shawn was still listed.

"Your father is still there? Hey, start a new season with the Lions."

Job scrolled past the screens. "The record is the same. It seems stuck on the Lions. It's broke… I'm going to restart it, so we can just play against each other."

Job started to reach for the power button, but Disney gently tackled his hand with hers to stop him. Pleasantly startled by her touch, Job took a quick deep breath, smiled, and began to stare into her eyes. Disney, entranced by the game, never returned his loving gaze. Instead, she snatched her hand away and grabbed a controller.

"No, let's play together. Let's play the schedule… I mean… I don't want to play *against* you all the time. I want to be on the same team," Disney explained.

Something about the word 'together' made Job smile. He took that word, "together", the feeling it evoked, and moved towards Disney. As he plopped down next to her on the sofa Disney and Job's eyes met. Sunbeams and moonbeams until this moment had never been seen in the same place at the same time. In her eyes he saw the moon. In his eyes she saw the sun. Without breaking the fantastic flood of moonbeams that shot from her eyes to his and the enormous effusion of sunbeams that shot from his eyes to hers, they began to fold space an inch at a time. He saw in her a place to rest. In his eyes she saw a place to live.

Job clutched her hand and a few seconds that seemed to last for a thousand forevers. Disney did not withdraw. She returned Job's clutch. But then a twitch, a hesitation, by Disney. Job felt a withdrawal. Maybe it was a readjustment. Maybe Disney's nose was itching and she really needed to scratch it. Maybe she had to sneeze. Got a chill. Or maybe, just maybe, it all hit her at once. The thought of walking down the school hall holding hands with Job, taking prom photos, choosing wedding cakes, homes, cars, insurance plans, and baby clothes. Whatever it was, it was enough of a flitch, twitch or sign, singular, to hit Job like two Cher-sized *Moonstruck* slaps, plural. Job released his grasp and snapped out of it. `

"I need my revenge, woman," Job playfully growled, as he tried once again for the power button.

This time Disney blocked his hand with her foot. They noticed at the same time that her shoe was untied.

Disney flashed her soft brown eyes his way. "Job..." she whispered, "... we may never see each other again. I want our last times together to be filled with memories of having fun together, not fighting."

Job grumbled to cover the sound of his beating heart. He didn't know if it kicked up because of the soft sound of her voice or the fact that what she said might very well be true. Instead of restarting the game, he tied Disney's shoe. Having tied shoes since he was two years old, it seemed like an easy enough task, but his hands did not move as efficiently as usual. Perhaps it was the wave of nervous crush anxiety coursing through his veins. If Disney had noticed, she did not mention it, thank goodness. He looked up and found her smiling.

Was that another moment? Disney thought to herself. It felt like maybe they had just had a moment, but she did not know for sure.

Job snapped to his feet with a swift harshness. "Well… who are you going to play?"

Disney's eyes narrowed with suspicion. *It was ANOTHER moment!* She picked up the controller. Her first executive decision was to remove Shawn from the Trading block. Glancing over, she caught Job's smile.

"Smart move," Job uttered.

"I thought so."

Job moved to the Franchise Menu and clicked on the Lions. A runner appeared on the bottom of the screen that said, "Game in Progress, Join, Press X."

Job looked at Disney and shrugged. "We doing this or what?"

Bolstered with confidence, Disney nodded her head. "Oh yeah."

Job pressed X and the game began. The Lions were down by thirty-four.

Disney chuckled at the impossible situation. "Oh! A thirty-four point deficit. Two quarters."

"Just throw me the damn ball," Job said.

"Alright Keyshawn."

As they played, Al Michaels gave a play by play in a voiceover. A wide receiver went in motion, which left room for Branson to run the sideline. Shawn dropped back. Branson shot up the field. The safety doubled the wide receiver, and he stopped. Shawn pumped fakes to the wide receiver. The safety took the bait and tried to make a play on the ball. The safety moved to recover, but Branson was wide open.

"I'm open! I'm open!" Job yelled.

Shawn threw the ball. It slid into Branson's hands, and he ran to the end zone. Disney and Job gave each other pounds and high fives.

"See, we're a better team together," Disney proclaimed.

"That's only seven."

Disney glanced over her shoulder where the real game was playing on the other television screen. "Ahh… Job look."

Something in her tone caught his attention. He half-expected to discover a giant spider dangling from the ceiling when he whirled around on his heels. "What?"

"The Lions, Branson just scored!"

Disney and Job's mouths dropped like their bottom lips were synchronized base jumpers. Then the windows to their souls widened as each contemplated what they both knew could most definitely not be happening in an unmagical Universe such as theirs. No words, just pauses, as Disney waited for Job—and Job waited for Disney—to say what they both were thinking.

"What? Nah… just a coincidence," Job denied it but his eyes grew wide as the instant replay showed that Madden and the real Lions' game had just had an identical series of movements.

Disney did not believe it was more than a coincidence any more than he did. But yet the possibility left her bursting with a newfound energy, and she rushed, "Let's get this ball back."

As they continued to play the video game, Disney tried to steal quick peeks at the other television, and each time Job chided her. "I can't help it, Job. It's unbelievable! Everything we do, they do!"

A hot rush of air expelled from Job's lips, half-whistle, half-groan. It was the best he could conjure at the moment. Caught in a frenzy, Job felt the pressure almost as if it was him standing on the field. The pressure to perform was exceeded only by the pressure to disbelieve what he was seeing. "It's uncanny. I'll give you that," Job said incredulously.

Denial ain't just a river in Egypt. And when it came to

belief, hope, and positive thinking, Job and Disney were much like the two tributaries of the world's longest river. Job was the Blue Nile and Disney the White Nile. The moniker and all that came with it couldn't have been more apropos, absent it being called the Honolulu Blue Nile, after the Lions' color, which also included silver, black, and white. However, it would be just as unlikely that a river in Africa would be named even in part after a city in the Pacific Islands.

Job, much like the portion of the river for which he was a tributary, responded too harsh and arid seasons and droughts in the same way: by drying up. In Job's case he simply stopped believing. Even when witnessing his dreams becoming a reality he refused to believe, for fear that once he accepted something good he would wake up and it would be taken away.

"You don't think…" Disney said cautiously.

And Disney, like the White Nile that gets its name from the river's clay sediment, was a flowing foundation of hope and optimism that thrived in any environment. Turn the heat up and she would be beautiful clay art. Turn the heat down and she would pour life into all those that encountered her.

"I don't know. They were down by thirty-four before we started playing and now they are back in the game," Job replied.

Disney grabbed Job's hand and nodded yes. Without saying a word, she gave him permission to surrender to the belief and the possibility of being hurt or happy.

"I don't know what's happening, but if we stop playing, they might too! We're just gonna focus on us," Job explained, as he chose a dime double wide receiver defense.

Equally invested in both comforting Job and in maintaining the Lions' momentum, Disney's brow crinkled in a frown. "No, Job. It's the end of the third quarter."

"You're right," he conceded, then they looked at each other and yelled in unison, "They're running!"

As the Defense lined up on Ford Field, Disney selected a Defensive Tackle on Madden.

"No, no, no," Job said. "Get the Middle Linebacker. Let the tackle clog the middle and we…"

"Rush from both sides," Disney finished for him.

A linebacker is creeping up. There's the snap. OH! IT'S A JAILBREAK. The linebackers are storming across the line. The quarterback doesn't have time to hand the ball off. He's scrambling. He's looking to throw it away. Got it off but got touched up on the release. It's a wounded duck! It's floating in the air. That ball has some hangtime! Oh, 6'1 205lbs of safety aka Damon Brock, no relation to Rolando Brock batted it up in the air. Well, at least his fingertips did. Oh it's coming down. He's juggling it! Juggling it! Juggling it!

"And it's intercepted!" Michaels exclaimed.

"Block!" Disney shouted.

Disney moved from side-to-side. Damon dodged tacklers. He spun, juked, and even plowed over a receiver. With only one final obstacle, a three hundred-pound Center that somehow rumbled into Damon's path. Job's hands manipulated the controller. BAM! A linebacker cleaned the Center's clock with a block from the shoulder, which sent the center flying out of bounds into the Powerade stand. Damon dove into the end zone.

"Savage," Disney murmured in admiration.

Watch! Take a look at this here. Boom! He got hit by a truck! Madden said from the television screen.

…

For over 15 minutes, Disney and Job spoke the universal language understood by every being from homo sapiens to insects: silence. It's a living language that after a while grows into a person. After 20 minutes, that silence matured into a person and sat down between Job and Disney as each held their controllers and stared at the screen. Stared at the box score: Raven 42, Lions 49. Disney grew tired of speaking and sharing the room with silence and decided to speak up, in American. Detroiter to be exact.

"What up doc?" Disney chortled at him.

"Really, you gonna act like you just got here," Job laughed.

Disney smiled. As Job stared at her, his laugh became a giggle, a smile, and finally a sigh.

"So now what? What's the play?" Job uttered with solemnly raised eyebrows.

"Well, when in doubt, I play zone. I'm a defensive mastermind. But we aren't on defense. Feel like we're on offense. You tell me. What should we do?"

He stared off into the distance and his mind went with him. His micro expressions trotted through an emotional corridor of suffering, hurt, and fear also known as memory lane. Within a blink he then turned his attention to his present. He looked over his shoulder, around half the home that he had created as a solvent for his wound.

As he turned to scan the other half, his eyes settled upon Disney. As she eyed him back, Job nodded slightly with the determination of prey that made the evolution jump to apex predator. What should we do? No. Those eyes inspired more. No longer afraid of life, he embraced his new role and recast the question. *What would you do to keep me? Protect us?*

"Everything, absolutely every fuckin' thing."

"I think in the NFL knowledge is power, and you try to get the knowledge by whatever means."
~Steve Sabol, President and Co-Founder of NFL Films

"Feels good, doesn't it?"

Startled, Cleo jumped in her seat and discovered Billie Wall standing beside her in the overpopulated owner's box. Tip had introduced Billie and her husband, Stan, who she had met previously which is a whole other story just before the game. They had both seemed unassuming compared to the usual but unusually varied cast of the characters he paraded in-and-out of the box.

She was clearly in Detroit, but you wouldn't know it by the Vegas vibe, minus the busy carpet designed to make you stare at your surroundings rather than the floor. No, the Lions' box was much like all its suites. Blue carpet that was so low that it required little maintenance. Theater seating for those that wanted to watch the game. A few feet behind them, tables with luxurious and stain-resistant chairs. Plush but not so much that it could not be easily maintained.

As she scanned the room, Cleo realized two things. One, she understood what it meant to be alone in a crowd. Well, alone until Billie, *think that's her name,* crossed to the schoolyard and offered to play. In the process she revealed that she, like Cleo, in this mostly male, mostly white, all wealthy motley crew of box attendees, was the living personification of touchdown being yelled at a basketball game. Oh and two, that part of her new position - *owner* - entailed remembering names and faces. Mind you she hadn't yet decided to be or not to be. An owner that is. Neither Tip's question nor money had been answered or returned. *And what the hell was Tip's position anyway?*

As she scanned the room, Cleo was certain she would have better luck memorizing the periodic table. Her mind sidetracked just long enough to make her forget what Billie had just said that had startled her in the first place. "I'm sorry. What's that?"

Billie sat down in the seat next to Cleo's. "Winning — it feels good, doesn't it?"

"Well," Cleo chuckled. "It certainly feels better than losing. I mean… for the fans' sake. I'd hate for them to pay money and have to watch their favorite team lose. You're Billie Wall, the coach from Tennessee, right?"

Billie side-eyed Stan and Tip as they stood within earshot and pretended they were not ear-hustling her conversation with Cleo. Billie's outward expression remained unchanged as inwardly she cringed. Stan had issued very concise and direct marching orders. He would work the Tip angle while she schmoozed the new owner, who by all accounts knew next-to-nothing about the game. Considering Stan had shown no hesitation stretching the truth, why should she? "Actually, we coach together as a team."

Cleo nodded in delight. Unbeknownst to Cleo, Billie silently gauged her reaction. Football was a lot like the game of life. If you want to win, you have to be willing to take risks. Stan believed that Tip held the only door into the Lions' organization, but Billie was willing to bet against it. "Don't worry. Your secret's safe with me," Billie playfully whispered.

"My secret?"

"It's gotten to you—football, I mean. It gets in your blood, quickly, you know," Billie explained.

A hesitant smile lifted Cleo's lips. Billie was proving to be a pleasant surprise. "I believe you are confused. This is the part where you tell me that I am too young, too incompetent, and how it would be in my best interest to sell."

"I don't know..." Billie's attention was suddenly captured by the game on the field. "Shoulder block," she grunted to no one in particular. The entire owner's box, much like a choir, let out a collective harmonious, "Ooh!"

Cleo looked below trying to see what Billie was talking about, but all she saw was a bunch of men running every which-a-way... then... one flying through the air and landing inside the Powerade stand. "Oh my," she gasped.

At the same moment, Billie jumped from her seat. "YEAH!"

Cleo looked up at Billie and started laughing.

Billie sat back down in her seat and then cleared her throat. "Like I was saying...the new coach,.... isn't looking bad... I suppose. The players are definitely finding their rhythm, it seems to me that if you sell now, it would be like leaving the party just when it was getting started."

Cleo had to clamp her lips tight to keep her mouth from gaping open. Since she had arrived on the scene, Cleo had been made to feel like the ultimate party crasher. Tip might have been the most vocal, but he wasn't a lone renegade in the *Sell, Cleo, Sell Campaign*. "Do you really feel that way?"

Just like reeling in a big fish. Only in this instance, Billie had to convince the fish that she was, in fact, a fish. "Life's too short to say things you don't mean."

Billie had made a career out of reading players' eyes. Cleo wasn't much different. Her eyes were filled with uncertainty but also an underlying determination. If Billie had to bet, which in a way she was, she'd be willing to wager that Cleo was the kind of woman who liked to prove people wrong.

"The thing is…" Cleo leaned forward. When Billie followed suit, she continued with a whisper, "…I don't have a good vibe about the new coach."

Billie's eyes flared with surprise. "Why? Are you unhappy with his style? The way he treats the players?"

Cleo looked around nervously, which she knew was ridiculous. Technically speaking, she was *the BO$$*. If only she had a pair of big girl boss panties with a matching boss bitch bra, the kind you only had to pull up/put on and be instantly blessed with confidence and swagger. A slight grimace curled her lips caused by the thought of becoming an AXE body spray commercial. Memories of middle school when the boys doused themselves with it filled her mind. "No, nothing like that. I really couldn't tell you much about his style. This is the first time I have watched him coach."

Billie pulled back in her seat. She looked at Cleo, nodded wordlessly and then waited for more. When Cleo said nothing, Billie tilted her chin down and raised her eyebrows, beckoning for Cleo to go on.

And just like clockwork, Cleo eagerly delivered. "*What?*"

Billie sighed as she ran her hand through her tousled hair. Though her pixie-cut looked sharp on the odd day when she bothered styling it, she had chosen the cut as nothing more than a measure of convenience, and today her sporty look illustrated that point well. "Given the circumstances, it was a tough decision for you."

Cleo rolled her eyes in frustration. "If you want to call it that. My decision was just a formality because Tip had already given him a short-term contract. Here's the real kicker, no one said a damn thing to me. It was like I wasn't even in the room."

Billie gritted her teeth as she shook her head with disgust.

"Honestly?" Cleo exclaimed. "How have you managed to breathe so long in this testosterone cloud without choking to death?"

Billie stared at Cleo for a microsecond but it felt like a micro millennium for Cleo. Then she burst into laughter, and Cleo began to giggle.

"For starters, I take the field as a coach, not as a person or woman. And to be real honest, I've had my fair share of naysayers along the way. I've had to work twice as hard just to prove myself to receive half the credit. I learned all the ins and outs, the most minute details, because I knew there would always be someone waiting to trip me up. I decided a long time ago that I wasn't going to give them the satisfaction."

"I..." Cleo paused, looking dazed and overwhelmed, which was just what Billie wanted.

"You're worried about the wrong game." Billie responded. "If football the game and football the business were the same, there would be no NFL. You need to worry more about how the game of business is played rather than football."

Cleo nodded and leaned in.

"It's not brain surgery, and you're a smart person. You just need to get the right person in your corner to show you the ropes. This may be a man's game, but now you are a very important part of it. They either need to accept that fact or get out of your way."

On the other side of the owner's box, Tip stood with Stan and a few others. Everyone's full attention was on the game below except Tip's. Things certainly seemed to take an unexpected upswing below, but, for now, Tip was concerned about the surprise plays in the box. He was too far away to hear, so he began eye-hustling.

He pulled Stan away from the others and then motioned towards Cleo and Billie. "That could be a problem."

Stan shook his head in denial. "Billie knows what she is doing."

"I'm sure she does, but do you?"

Outrage flickered in Stan's eyes. Tip's implication would have been just as well received if he had dared claim that Billie had been unfaithful, but Stan remembered who he was talking to. "Billie would never."

"Yeah…" Tip murmured sounding less than convinced. "…I'm sure Samson said the same thing to Delilah."

...

Later that evening, Cleo sat cross-legged on the floor in the middle of her studio apartment. It was ridiculous to think that she was an NFL owner yet still lived in an apartment that was appropriate for a poor, struggling college student. Until Tip had entered her life a few weeks ago, she had been very comfortable with her unmapped future.

After crash-coursing into adulthood, she was finally starting to accept the fact that her days as a free-spirit were over. Her decisions now directly impacted the lives and livelihoods of others. At some point, she had to stop listening to people—notably Tip, who clearly did not have her best interests at heart—and start trusting her own intuition.

Cleo wanted to win both on and off the field. Since she had no idea where to begin, she did the only thing she knew to do. She Googled. In fact, she Googled her ass off! Cleo found several impressive articles about Stan Wall, but she did not care about the numbers, or honestly, too terribly much about Stan. She was far more curious about his wife, Billie. Unfortunately, the sports writers had very little to say about her, but she suspected a few of Billie's former players just might. They were easy enough to find on Instagram and much to her delight incredibly responsive. Her DM inquiries were returned almost as soon as she hit send. Cleo smirked as she thought and felt that sometimes, even if it was in name only, it was good to be an owner.

...

Cleo woke to the sound of her phone vibrating. She flickered open her eyes with a squint and an expression of dismay, and looked at her night stand clock. It was seven o'clock in the morning. She picked up her phone, saw that it was Tip, hit ignore, tossed the phone back on the nightstand, and rolled back over to go sleep.

After he called her for the fifth straight time, she begrudgingly answered, "What do you want?"

"Turn on *Sports Center*," Tip demanded.

"I don't want to," Cleo countered.

"I don't care. Just turn it on."

Cleo reached for the remote and flipped on the TV. Cari Champion, ESPN reporter filled her screen.

Well, folks, this is something you don't hear about every day. It seems last night was a busy one for Cleo White, the new owner of the Detroit Lions...

A screenshot of her Instagram following was flashed on the television.

While the rest of us were sleeping, Cleo was friending players from all over the league. This leaves us with so many questions. What does this mean for the future of the Lions? Can we expect owner IG updates on Sundays? Is this what happens when a millennial takes over a NFL team? Is this tampering? Is Cleo the new Jerry Jones? Most importantly, why didn't you follow me? Cleo, if you're listening, please call and explain.

"Do you have any idea what you have done?" Tip gritted into the phone. "There are protocols, guidelines, specific ways things are done."

"Yeah, about that..." Cleo paused to yawn, "...I fired your coach last night."

"You what!" Tip growled.

Cleo heard him take several deep breaths, which she surmised were supposed to be intimidating but instead reminded her of ocean wave sounds on her noise-maker.

"I have had nothing but your best interests in mind, but if you are going to make a laughing stock out of yourself and this team, then you are on your own," Tip said.

"Oh, shut the fuck up, Tip," Cleo exclaimed and ended the call. She stared at her phone with a scowl waiting for it to light up with a defiant Tip on the other end. Nothing happened. Cleo cracked a smile that would put a Minion to shame. However Cleo was destined to be no one's minion anymore. She was a muthafucking boss!

"In a crisis, don't hide behind anything or anybody. They're going to find you anyway."
~Bear Bryant, Head Coach, Alabama Crimson Tide Football Program

"Come on, Disney! You are going to be late for school," Debbie Landover yelled from somewhere downstairs.

"In a minute..." Disney hollered as she plopped down on the end of her bed and stared at the television set, which was playing ESPN's *Get Up!* morning show.

On this morning's edition, Jalen Rose was arguing with Ryan Clark. Disney walked out of her bathroom just in time to hear Smith say, *This is typical of the Lions. They win a game in grand fashion and fire the coach. After they lost a coach who walked off the field and said he would rather give up five million than coach this team. So now...*

Jalen countered, *Michael... my brotha... I'm a b-ball player... when I was younger we used to play this football game called, Pick'em up Mess'em up. Basically you run the ball and everyone tries to tackle you. There is no typical game of Pick'em up Mess'em up. You never know how it will go. And that's how I feel about the Lions. Typical went out the window the minute Cleo White came into the play. Contrary to all the speculations, she doesn't seem like someone who is looking to sell anytime soon. It's anyone's guess, but now that the Lions have shown what they can do, they can get a coach with real talent interested in them. Say, someone like Stan Wall.*

"Disney..." Debbie sighed as she barged into Disney's room.

"I'm coming."

"Woah..." Debbie exclaimed as Disney stood up. "Hmm... you want to explain what this is about," she said as she pointed towards Disney.

Disney crossed her arms over her chest defensively. "It's nothing."

"Okay, well contrary to what you believe, I haven't always been thirty-two years old. Once, a million years ago, I was your age, but I don't remember a visit from the Titty Fairy and waking up one morning with C-cups."

Disney groaned as she tucked her head. "Mom... it's just a little padding. Don't make it a thing."

Debbie walked across the room and gently reached for Disney's face. "And what's this? Are you wearing mascara?"

Mortified, Disney tried to shrug past her mother. Any other morning, Debbie would have had her face stuck in her phone scrolling through Facebook or worse...updating Snapchat. Her mom didn't understand that she was a little too old for golden butterflies or puppy face filters. "Come on, I don't want to be late to school."

Debbie sat down on Disney's bed and then motioned for Disney to sit beside her. "This is more important. School can wait."

Seriously... with a stubborn scoot, Disney moved towards the bed and sat down. "I'm not a little girl anymore."

Debbie stroked Disney's hair. "I know that you are becoming a beautiful young woman, and one day you will be an absolute knockout, but you don't need to rush it."

Disney moved out of Debbie's reach and crossed her arms over her padded chest in defiance. "You don't get it. Kids are different now. Maybe in your day, the girls still carried *My Little Mermaid* backpacks to high school, but they don't now. Most of the girls in my grade have boyfriends… and they do sh—"

Disney caught herself and stuffed that curse word under her tongue. "They do stuff, Mom."

Debbie sat up tall as she ran her perfectly manicured fingernails through her highlighted beach waves that reached the middle of her spine. Disney silently pondered that *maybe* her mother was not the best person to give lectures about enhancements. Disney knew for a fact that Debbie had gotten a nose job and lip injections. In her defense, Debbie claimed that she had the procedures years ago before she was a mother, and her priorities had since changed. In fact, Disney faintly recalled her mom having the lip implants removed or as Disney sarcastically called it unimplanted. *Whatever…* now Debbie was into cupping and ate avocados like they were fruits from the Gods. When she wanted a treat, she might slide a piece of toast under her self-proclaimed *'cados.*

"For your information, back in my day the kids would sneak liquor from their parents' cabinet and pass it around the locker room like candy. *And,* one of my best friends got pregnant at the end of eighth grade, which by the way, if you do either of those things you will be grounded until you are thirty-five. The only reason I mentioned it is because you seem to believe I grew up in cotton candy land. So… stuff? Stuff like kissing?"

Disney looked back at her mom with eyes as big as saucers. She could feel another talk coming on. She was still more shook from the first one than the shook ones mentioned in the song aptly named *Shook Ones Part II* by Mobb Deep. That song, according to Complex, ranks 23 of 25 of the most violent rap songs of all time. That said, added padding to bras had nothing on bringing alcohol to school. "Kissing… and stuff."

Debbie sighed. Just a few years ago Disney had still

believed in Santa Claus and the Tooth Fairy. Now they had to have a conversation about penetration… and not the kind you find in football. "And is this boy interested in the *and stuff* part?"

"MOM," Disney gasped as her face burned red with embarrassment. "I never said I liked anyone…especially a boy."

"You didn't have too. Girls don't start stuffing bras without a boy in mind. Or maybe… I suppose, another girl in mind."

"Oh. My. God. You seriously, *did not* just ask me if I am gay."

Debbie held out her hands in a defensive posture. "You said it! Kids are different these days. They are a lot more open about these things. That's a good thing."

Reeling from the conversation, Disney missed the flicker of sadness that passed through Debbie's eyes. "It's nothing like that. First off, I'm not gay. If was I would tell you and I would out AF! Second, we are just friends. I thought maybe… you know… he might see me as something else."

Debbie pulled Disney into her arms and gathered her close. "At your age, boys and girls are so different. In fact, the difference never really goes away, no matter how old you are, but my gut instinct says if this boy is a friend… maybe even a really good friend… he already likes you—just the way you are now. And if you want to start wearing make-up, bras, and all the other girlie stuff, I will take you shopping. We'll find the best shades for your complexion, and I can teach you how to put it on, but… Remember Disney, we are doing this for you. You don't ever need to change a single thing about yourself just to make someone else happy. I know you won't ask your dad, so ask Job, he's a boy. I can't believe I'm actually trying to get a teenager to cosign my advice. He will tell you the same thing."

Disney chuckled.

"Yeah, Mom, I'll ask Job. You're so perceptive."

"Yes, yes I am."

Disney and Debbie both smiled and shot each other *a wait do you know that I know or think you know what I know but don't know for sure.* Yeah, that confusing type of glance.

...

Damon bounced up and down on his feet inside the Lions' practice field. "Man... it must be the new weight training regimen, I feel... I don't know... more..."

Rolando sauntered across the field with a bit more pep in his step. "Powerful?"

"*Yeah*! Just strong. I don't know whom to thank, the strength coach or the nutritionist, but both of them got Christmas gifts coming. Christmas, Kwanzaa, Hanukkah...all that shit!"

They both laughed.

Rolando pounded his fist against his chest. "No man... I feel you. I woke up this morning feeling the same. It's like I have this energy... like crazy Hulk energy... like I'm about to burst into a giant green monster."

Shawn walked over just in time to hear the end of Rolando's testimony. "Alright, good. I was thinking it was just me."

"You feeling it too?" Damon asked while riding his invisible pogo stick.

Shawn's expression grew stern. "Yeah... different. I do feel more confident. I can't explain it."

"But did y'all see the twins? They go through some sort of second puberty? You see it, right? It isn't just me, right? They're taller," Damon asked without missing a bounce.

"What are you talking about, Damon? They went to see the chiropractor. For some reason they both got over their fear of having their backs cracked. And why you keep jumping up and down? You got to go to the bathroom or something?" Shawn asked as he stole breaths between his howls and roars of laughter.

Rolando positioned himself in a front double bicep pose and then looked over his arms to see if he ripped out the practice gear. "No man... I see it too. It makes me feel so... like I want to ROAR."

"Get it together," Shawn chided. "Hey, is that Stan Wall?"

At once, the team walked over and huddled around Stan. No one seemed to notice that both Billie and Cleo had come on the field with him and that they had just been shut out... no one except Cleo and Billie.

"This is great, great, great!" Damon yelled.

Billie leaned over and whispered to Cleo, "Don't ever be afraid to remind them who you are. People have a tendency to forget things like that on the field."

"Gentleman," Cleo said in her most authoritative voice, which went completely unnoticed.

"Man, I hoped it would be you," Rolando said.

Stan held up his hands and tried to explain, but the team was hearing none of it.

"You were my first choice," Tracy exclaimed.

A piercing, shrill whistle shattered the joviality. Billie's whistle. All eyes turned towards the two ladies. Billie looked at Cleo as if to pass the floor to her. Finding herself in the sudden spotlight, Cleo's brain froze.

"Hi guys," she said meekly and glanced in Billie's direction. Even with the whistle still between her lips, Cleo could see the grimace on Billie's face.

"Okay...so yeah..." Cleo started and she cleared her throat, "... I have invited the Walls here today. As sometimes happens, my vision of this team's direction and the previous coach's vision were not in tune, and we have respectfully parted ways. I may not know a lot about football, but I do know that every team needs consistency. Before any more hasty decisions are made, I have invited them to run a practice, and they have graciously agreed. It's not normal, but most exciting things aren't. So... with that being said, I will leave you to it."

Billie avoided Stan's probing glare as she was certain he hadn't missed the 'them' and 'they'. Billie grunted with authority, "Okay boys... you heard the lady. First thing—tackling for everyone!"

Cleo walked towards the sidelines and was surprised when Stan fell in step beside her. She looked back over her shoulder and pointed towards the players. "Oh… aren't you…"

Stan waved his hand in dismissal. "She's just adjusting the finer points while I assess the player's strengths and weaknesses."

"I would have thought that was what film footage was for."

At that moment, Stan realized that Cleo wasn't nearly as naive as Tip had let on.

"This whole new coach trial practice is a bit unorthodox," Stan said.

His lips pressed together in a grim frown as he glanced across the field towards his wife. Her assessment of Cleo's character was equally dismissive. In fact, on the flight up, Billie had predicted that Cleo would go along with anything Tip said. Stan was beginning to think they were both wrong.

"Nothing beats seeing live action," Stan muttered nervously.

After several minutes of directing the practice, Billie reached for Tracy's helmet. "You don't swipe at the legs. You wrap them up and hold them."

"I'm a running back. I don't have to tackle." Tracy attempted to scuttle away quickly with a look of *did I say that out loud* splashed across his face.

He refused to meet Billie's gaze. Before he could escape, she pulled on his helmet, and he pushed her hand away. Her eyebrow cocked up. *You're lucky you aren't one of my boys.* If he were, Billie would have ripped him a new one, but instead she looked past the sullen, little brat until her eyes landed on Damon. *"Pogo Boy."*

"Please not me, please not me, please…" Damon whispered.

"Damon, spring your way down here. You're playing running back… and Tracy is the linebacker… I mean if you think you can handle that."

Tracy shook his head with disgust and the Twins started to laugh. Billie snapped her fingers and the Twins fell silent. "You're right," she said, pointing in their direction. "Never send a boy to do a woman's job. Traci, with an "i"… *you're* the running back."

Damon sighed with relief while the rest of the team looked befuddled. He tried to slip away unnoticed, but Billie's whistle brought him to an abrupt halt. "Pogo Man, I like your enthusiasm even if I'm not convinced you would be able to pass a piss test at the moment… or in a week for that matter. Come play tight end."

Damon glared at Billie. She returned a glower of her own. The dance of dirty looks was on. Stan watched with clenched fists hoping this would escalate. He began rehearsing the script. Got so into it that he started mumbling the words, "Billie it's not me but the players have complained… yada yada." However, before his smile could reach its apex, it turned into a frown as Billie and Damon's dirty-looks-two-stepped into glares and words of respect. Words he had never heard used in reference to Billie rather than himself.

"I like you. I like you a lot, Coach Wall!" Damon said as he assumed his position.

"I would love to see myself as a head coach someday. I know some people might think it's crazy but, back in the day, if you would have said that women were going to play with the same rules as men do, they would have thought that was crazy. Being a head coach to me is being a teacher and I think we would never question whether men would listen to a woman as a professor."
~Katie Sowers, Coach, San Francisco 49ers

Disney stepped inside Shawn's living room and discovered Job with his eyes and hands glued to the PlayStation. "Have you been doing that all day? I wondered and our teachers, plural, wondered why you were absent."

Job cast Disney a quick side-eye and then, seemingly against his own will, found himself doing a double take. A perplexed frown crossed his brows. *Dayum, she looks good! Maybe I do need to take a break?* "You aren't going to believe this."

Disney sauntered over with a light sashay. "What?"

Job's expression grew more concerned. "You sick or something? You sound nasally? You want a cough drop?"

"*No*… just never mind." A barely audible sigh escaped her lips. "So, what am I not going to believe?"

"You look nice today," Job burst out suddenly, surprising them both.

"What did you say?"

"Nothing." Job fumbled with the remote.

"Never mind, it doesn't matter. Do you see this? I mean do you see this?" he exclaimed, as he began scrolling through the screens. "Not only does it list the free agents, but it lists people who have never played football. It has track athletes, boxers, MMA fighters..."

Disney was much more interested in the *nothing* part, but she knew Job wouldn't say any more... for now. "Click on that," she demanded as she pointed towards the Personnel screen. "Oh, it's the same with personnel. You can choose anybody all the way down to 1A."

"But, even better..." Job added, half in disbelief. "We can edit the players. The edit function on this is really detailed. We can edit regular Madden functions like carrying, strength, and all that... we can also edit players' weight, height, and even confidence."

Disney's eyes grew wide. "If this works... I mean..."

Job chuckled. He was still just as shocked by the discovery as he was when he had made it a few hours ago. "I know. It's all in your eyes. I can see what you're trying to say... okay, all you need to do is save it."

Disney closed her eyes and took a deep breath.

"You know, Job, most buttons are just buttons. They turn things on and off. But, every so often, there comes along a button that, when pushed, has the ability to turn the world upside down, inside out, round and round the other muthafuckin' way!"

Disney and Job stared at each other, seeing a future in each other's eyes when their lips met. Without breaking their gaze...

"Did you hear what I said? I'm so deep right now."

"So deep," Job said, mirroring her simpering.

They laughed and resumed the gaze.

"Do it," Job whispered.

Click.

...

"WHAT," Tracy exclaimed with his arms flailed wide. He marched straight towards Stan Wall. "This *ain't* happening!"

Cleo cocked her head to the side. With a sickening sweet voice, she murmured, "Tracy, what seems to be the problem?"

"OH NO!" Tracy bellowed. "No, no, no... ain't happening," he chanted as his wide eyes swung back and forth between Cleo and Stan. "You need to get a handle on your girl...," Tracy spat as he pointed towards Cleo, "...before this one turns your practice, fuck that team, into a pink, taco-hat wearing, hashtag movement."

Cleo was momentarily paralyzed by his rash display of emotion until she saw Billie silently marching towards them looking very much like a lion who was about to handle her cub, even if it meant sinking her teeth into his neck and dragging him back on the field. In comparison, Stan remained motionless, taking the strong/silent type to the next level.

"Tracy, perhaps it would be best to remember who it is you are talking to," Billie growled.

Cleo's eyes met Billie's over the irate player standing between them. Billie silently nodded, and Cleo realized this was her cue. Cleo gulped. She wanted to be a lion too but... "Tracy, just because she is a woman..."

"She ain't no woman. She's my fiancée."

"Okay," Cleo nodded. "I appreciate your concern for her welfare, but if Billie feels that she is capable..."

"Her welfare," Tracy scoffed, as he began pacing back-and-forth. "If she is fool enough to run around with the big boys, then she's got what's coming to her. This isn't about her. This is about me... and every other man on this field. Do you have any idea how this makes us look?"

Oh no the fuck he didn't. Much to her surprise, Cleo discovered that channeling her inner lion wasn't nearly as difficult as she had imagined. Her expression grew cold and unyielding. "The field isn't the place to deal with your male ego. After practice, I can give you the name and number of a good therapist I know though."

Across the field, Shawn leaned down and whispered to Traci, "Dang... I didn't know she had it in her."

"Me either."

"But the real question is... do *you* have it in you to take those hits?" Shawn asked.

Traci tried to catch her fiancé's glance. She didn't know if Tracy was just being Tracy, or if he really believed the crazy things coming out of his mouth. Everybody, except maybe Cleo, knew Tracy spoke a lot of nonsense, most of which he didn't mean. Billie hadn't seemed too keen on his attitude either. Traci had seen the look in Billie's eyes when Tracy pushed her hand away.

It reminded her of the look her mama used to have whenever she talked back as a child, which wasn't that often because she had learned real fast what came after that look. If Stan was going to become head coach, Tracy was going to have to change his ways, otherwise Tracy would have a long, difficult road ahead of him. "I hope so," Traci said, rather pled, like a repeat felon at their sentencing.

Shawn nudged Traci's shoulder. "This ain't about him. You don't need his approval to make this your moment."

Billie marched back across the field. "Let's play!" Billie bellowed as she walked back towards the players.

Tracy realized the conversation was over. His jaw set with bitter disappointment as he looked over at Stan and then begrudgingly followed a few steps behind in silence. He had heard nothing but good things out of Tennessee about Stan, but were they ever wrong. A grown man letting his wife call the shots—he ought to know better. As for Stan's woman, Tracy refused to look at her when he walked past because she ought to know better too.

Shawn was right. Traci did not need his approval. He had not stood by her side all those years ago when she had had to fight the school board to be allowed to play on the men's high school wrestling and football teams. And again when she wanted to play gunner on kickoff returns.

He hadn't been there when she had had to fight for her college scholarship or to compete in martial arts competitions against men. The issue had never been about her ability. It was always her gender. She had gotten this far without his approval, but right now, it would sure be nice if she had it.

If she did, she could concentrate on the next twenty seconds instead of worrying what they might mean for the next six months, year, indefinite future. When she had proposed, Tracy had promised that he would always have her back. A sinking feeling in her stomach had told her that he meant it, as long as she didn't steal any of his glory. Then again… maybe Cleo was onto something. The field was not the place for therapy or relationship counseling.

…

The ball was snapped and handed to Traci. She stood in place as the offensive line blocked and tried to clear a hole. Traci looked left then right. Finally, a defensive end broke through, and then another. Her pupils focused sharply and a tenacious grin crept across her face. She spun to avoid a tackle. The defensive ends collided.

Damon rolled towards the left. The right end put a swim move on the left guard. Traci followed Damon to the right. The right end smashed through Damon in an attempt to get to Traci.

Traci hurdled to the right end. She dodged, spun, and faked tacklers. Her style was different. She stopped when you least expected and struck when you expected her to coil. Traci looked and moved like Barry Sanders, LaDainian Tomlinson, and Walter Payton all rolled into one. From the corner of her eye, she saw Tracy cutting across the field to stop her. Tracy had the angle. She couldn't go around him— she had to go through him.

In that moment, Tracy was no longer her fiancé. He was the one obstacle standing between her and her moment. Just as they were about to collide, she kicked it into third gear, and much to the amazement of everyone on field, Traci bulldozed him and dragged him ten yards into the end zone.

...

After all the players had left for the evening, Billie and Stan were gathered with Cleo in her office. "Well..." Cleo said brightly, "...that was certainly an interesting practice. Thank you very much for allowing me to watch..."

"But?" Billie prompted after Cleo's prolonged pause.

Cleo nodded. "But, I do have concerns."

"You aren't the only one," Stan supplied.

Cleo blinked with her surprise. "Oh," she murmured as she looked back and forth between husband and wife. "Please, Stan..." she said as she motioned towards him, "...what is your take?"

Stan glanced at Billie and then, leaning forward in his seat, he looked back at Cleo. "For starters, I have to question the wisdom of putting a five foot seven, one hundred and seventy, eighty pound girl..."

"Woman," Cleo gently corrected.

"Woman..." Stan conceded as he waved his hand, "...in the running back position. Hell, I'm not sure how she even became a kicker."

Cleo's expression grew studious as she mulled over

his concerns. After a moment, she countered, "Yet, she performed spectacularly."

Stan once again glanced at Billie. "I think it was obvious, and Billie will agree, that the team was holding back. Especially that little spectacle at the end."

"I don't know," Billie gritted through her teeth. "From my vantage point, it looked like Tracy was out for blood."

"The point is," Stan began and cleared his throat, "in a game day situation that can never happen. Traci is a football player, not a martyr for the #MeToo movement."

Cleo flashed a baffled look once she processed the misuse of the #MeToo. She raised a finger to speak but thought better of it. *Plus when someone is showing their call why not let them reveal the whole damn playbook?*

"The other team will pulverize her. She should only be used on special teams as a damn kicker….maybe."

Cleo nodded as her nails drummed on the table. "That's certainly something to consider. I suppose I am just a little surprised that you didn't mention this during practice. In fact, I don't entirely understand your role in this."

Inwardly, Stan cursed like a sailor. *I bet she might understand that.* Thirty years of hard work and sacrifice, and it all came down to explaining himself to a twenty-something, idealistic, entitled, rabble-rousing geriatric gen zer. Plain and simple, sometimes life just wasn't fair. "Well… I'm the head coach."

"Yet, it was your wife who ran the practice, made all the calls, and it was Billie who handled an irate player… all the while, you were standing back looking at the big picture."

"I suppose you might see it that way."

"So… my concern is that you don't see the problem in this," Cleo answered. "I would like to make an offer for the role of head coach, but it just makes the most sense to me to offer it to the person who is actually doing the damn job!

Billie..." Cleo paused as she reached inside her desk and retrieved the contract. She handed it to Billie. "I will give you a few days to look this over. Feel free to have an attorney review it for you. If you pass, Billie, I'm not going to hire Stan. I will move onto another candidate. If you like, you can bring him on as a coordinator. Give me your answer by the end of the week."

"We find it so odd when women lead men, but women have been teaching men for years. We have to normalize it."
~Katie Sowers, Coach, San Francisco 49ers

Stan and Billie rode in heavy silence the entire way to the airport. A sensory deprivation chamber was like a stadium concert compared to the silence filling the car. Once they reached the airport, the tension only seemed to get worse. They didn't speak a word, even during those little moments where you are supposed to say something, nod, help lift, and so forth. There was no need for a plane: the tension was so thick they could have rode it all the way home with enough left over to take 101 souls with them.

As they moved through the bustling midday crowd, Stan was recognized by a few diehard fans. He responded to their requests for photos and autographs with something between a grunt and bark. The diehards walked away empty-handed and disappointed.

"Where's your game face, Stan?" Billie whispered from the corner of her mouth.

...

Stan's dour expression remained etched upon his face despite the comfortable business class seats, and even despite being doted upon by an adoring flight attendant. His mood provided Billie little in the way of in-flight entertainment. So Billie reached for the pamphlets that were tucked behind the seat in front of her and managed to pass a few minutes alternating between thumbing through pamphlets and looking out the window. She did not want to initiate conversation, but she found both about as engaging as a soon-to-be-cancelled Netflix Original. Eventually, against her will, her tongue just started moving. "Are we going to talk about it?"

Stan sniffed with disgust. "I'm not sure what you want me to say. You let me down, Billie."

"*Excuse me*?"

"The way I see it, you either missed the call *or* you straight up lied to me."

Furious, Billie squeezed her hands together. She didn't know what was worse—being called incompetent or a liar. "I did everything you asked me to do. You were the one that said get us an offer. Well, guess what, that's what I did. It might not be the offer you wanted, but it is better than nothing."

Stan expelled a sarcastic chuckle. "A serious offer."

"It WAS a serious offer."

"You… you can't be serious," Stan scoffed.

"Why not?"

"Do you really believe that I have dedicated the last thirty years of my life to this game —to become Mr. Billie Wall, husband of the head coach? Besides, you aren't even head coach material."

Billie flinched as if she had just been slapped. She took a deep calming breath, that did not work. "What the fuck is that supposed to mean?" She was doing everything she could to convey her fury while still keeping her voice down, aware of nearby passengers.

Stan's eyes expanded to the size of iPad screens. Stan didn't need to ask which point of his argument offended her. Never mind what all this meant to his career. "You know very good and well what I mean. You're a hot head, Billie. You always have been. Today's practice was just another classic example. Tracy gave you a little attitude so you had to humiliate him. I don't care what you or that…. *owner* believes," —he raised his hands and emphasized Cleo's title using air quotes, "it was the *wrong* call. It's the kind of call that could ruin a career… or worse."

Billie's expression matched Stan's. *Mr. and Mrs. Grim.* She turned away and stared at the clouds.

...

"Hey Big Dog, you still at it?" Job yelled out.

Shawn pivoted on his heels with the football cradled in his arms. "Come on, let's go to the backyard," he answered and motioned for Job to join him in the Serengeti-sized backyard with a lawn large enough to play a 12 on 12 professional football game sans fans.

"You really want to do this?" Job teased as he walked over and crouched down in a three point stance. "Did they go easy on you in practice after last week's big game?"

"Nah…" Shawn uttered as he unhooked the ball from the strap, "… it was one of the hardest practices yet."

"But you still want more?" Job challenged and then took off running for fifty yards. Job cut left to the imaginary end zone. Shawn launched the ball, and Job dove forward and caught the ball.

Shawn's hands rose for the touchdown. "I feel it. Can you feel it, son? There is magic in the air."

Yes, I do. "Is that so?" He played it cool, but yes, something strange was definitely happening.

"Oh yeah," Shawn affirmed with a solid head nod. "I felt it in practice. This is going to be our season. *Mark my words.*"

...

Stan waited until Billie went back to the bedroom to likely watch the last episode of her latest Hulu Original before he returned Tip's call. Tip was not high on his priority list at the moment. In fact after today, returning Tip's call had moved into last place. But he couldn't put it off any longer.

"Stan, I've been trying to reach you all day. What the hell happened out there?" Tip demanded angrily.

Stan leaned back in his office chair. The desk in front of him was empty except for a laptop and a framed photograph of Billie and him taken 10 years ago on the deck of a cruise ship on their twentieth wedding anniversary. *What a team they were.* The photo had been sitting on the desk so long that he really didn't even notice it anymore. Stan flipped the frame over, and looked away as their smiles quickly vanished face down onto the desk, much as their once-romantic life had. "I was about to ask you the same question."

"Cleo's too young and inexperienced to know what she wants," Tip offered.

Stan glanced around his office. On every wall, in every nook and cranny, there were pieces, photographs and memorabilia, dedicated to his illustrious career. Never, not one single time, had he ever thought that he would come so close to the end zone, only to have the victory snatched from his grasp— by his own wife. Maybe in some ways, it might have been easier to swallow if she had simply stepped out with another man. Surely, it would not have felt as brutal as her betrayal on the field yesterday. "That's what everybody says, but she didn't seem that inexperienced to me, and Cleo made it obvious that she wanted my wife—not me."

"For now," Tip casually dismissed.

"What are you talking about?"

"Well… just think about it," Tip explained, "Billie is only in the position she is in because she has always had your foolishly unwavering support. She got to be the lioness because she always knew you would be the lion who had her back. What do you suppose would happen if she didn't have her crutch to lean on?"

Stan's surly frown deepened further. "What are you suggesting? That I leave the woman I have been married to for over thirty years?"

"My second wife once had mind to get a part-time job… until summer came around and she didn't get to spend as much time at the country club's pool. My point is, do you think I ever visited her at the hair salon, pet groomer, or wherever it was? No. I say, let Billie put on the big boy pants, and when she fails… and no doubt about it, without you, she *will* fail… Miss Cleo will come to her senses and realize you were the man for the job all along," Tip explained.

…

Job knew his dad was not teasing about feeling magic in the air. They went back inside and Shawn walked straight towards the kitchen. Given his father's career, Job had witnessed all sorts of victory dinners, from burger joints with a few of the other players and their families, through to extravagant sports banquets. But when Shawn really had the feels, nothing but a home-cooked meal would do.

Job hid a smile as memories of the times when his father would shoo his mother out of the kitchen and claim top chef status. And, heaven help them all if Day had any interest in the grill. Shawn could've put up with his wife on the field, or even in the locker room, but the grill? The grill was his last stand.

Tonight, it was breakfast for dinner. While his father was making a feast of omelettes French toast, pancakes—yes, pancakes and French toast—bacon, and sausage, Job flipped on the TV. *Around the Horn* was playing, and Job was not surprised that the Lions were the main topic of conversation.

Tony started the conversation. *Rumors, rumors, rumors. The Lions allegedly made history this morning by hiring the first female football coach and starting a woman at running back. Buy or sell these rumors?*

Bomani answered. *I've got to admit, I can't remember a time when the Lions received this much attention. They say she is young and inexperienced, but no one can deny that Cleo White is a conversation starter. Other NFL owners are mad they didn't think of it first. Still, I sell: this is not true. First, who has a coach come in to try out by running a practice? False, didn't happen. Second, it just simply can't be true. There is no way a woman can take the pounding that a running back takes. There is no way that a five-foot-five-inch-girl—pardon me, woman —is going to last a single play, let alone a game. Most running backs are washed at 30 because of the physical demands of the position. It's practically suicide for both the player and the franchise. It's just a publicity stunt for the Lions to get people out to the season opener. Third, Stan Wall is the coach!*

Tony awarded Bomani points for his sound argument and then he turned his attention to Jemele Hill. *What say you?*

Buy! Buy! Buy! We all know who was behind the success in Knoxville for the Walls. Now, we can see if she can do it in the NFL. If Traci with an "I" wants to replace her fiancé Tracy with a "Y" at running back, then I say good for her. Furth…

Tony muted Jemele. *That is enough from you, Jemele. The Supreme Court ruled that Maurice Clarett's body was not mature enough to play in the NFL. If a former Ohio State running back that left school early was not ready, how is a one hundred and I guess fifty pound female kicker going to do? Bottom line, she is an ok kicker but running up the middle ain't kicking since the ball doesn't kick back. Next topic.*

CHAPTER
14

"I think confrontation is healthy, because it clears the air very quickly."
~Bill Parcells, Head Coach, New York Giants

"You ready?"

Instead of answering yes or no, a nervous bubble of laughter slipped past Disney's lips.

Job's brow cocked up in confusion. "What?"

"I don't know. I'm just so nervous." Disney began pacing the length of Job's living room. While the movement did little to help her agitated nerves, she did like the feeling of the plush carpet squish between her toes. It reminded her of warm sand on a tropical beach.

Job shrugged. "There's nothing to be nervous about when you know you are going to win."

If that were true, she wouldn't feel this way now. "Then what?"

"Then... we win again... and again... and again," his voice diminished to an echo as he vacated the room.

"Hey," Disney yelled, "where are you going?"

Job peeked around a marble column that separated the living room from the foyer. "I need to make the game snacks. You take this one. Play it however you want to."

"You serious?" Disney gasped.

"You know I don't play about my snacks, woman…"

They laughed harder than two people in church that shouldn't laugh but couldn't fight it either.

...

"You look good in them pants," a lineman taunted.

In the I formation with Traci as running back, the Lions were seconds away from making history. Keeping that in mind, Traci knew that she could not let them get into her head. They wanted tears. They wanted to see her fail. Traci was not going to give them either.

Nodding towards the stands, she spat, "Why don't you say that to them."

The record-breaking season opening crowd was filled with signs bearing hashtags, posters, banners, and social justice content related to equality of race and gender.

"Those feminazis and snowflakes aren't going to save you when I take you down," another lineman called out.

Traci rolled her eyes at their trash talk, which bothered her mostly because it wasn't even good trash talk. It was whack af. Did they honestly believe they were the first players who had something to say about her wearing the uniform? She could give them the names of a few boys she remembered from high school. *Oh wait*—none of them had made it to the NFL. "And it isn't going to be your jersey that they can't keep in stock when you don't stop me. Don't feel bad. I'm sure after today you might be able to pick up an endorsement from the AARP."

Billie's shrewd eyes sliced through the stadium. Any rookie coach would be thrilled by the colossal reception, and she was no exception… if not for the media spin, which was already portraying her as some sort of ball-busting misandrist. Why was it so hard for people to understand that she not only had the skills, but she had fought hard and made sacrifices to earn her place at the table? Surely it was a big table with enough place settings for everyone? She had not gotten this far with the intention of snatching a seat out from anyone, yet not even her insolent, spoiled brat of a husband believed her. Why should they? She was a rookie.

Billie took no consolation in the fact that she was not the only one feeling the pressure. She glanced across the sideline where Tracy was moping with a stormy frown. She had half a mind to blow her whistle and remind him that it was just that sort of attitude problem that had got him replaced in the first place. Well, that and the fact that his fiancée was the better player and certainly more coachable, despite what Stan believed. It wasn't a *bad* call. It was the *only* call. Now, with the whole world watching, it was time for Traci to prove it.

Game time! There's the snap. Handoff to Traci Jones. Sweet Sassy Molassy! Landover just put a lineman on his back. Can't see who it is. He hit him so hard he erased his identity. Traci is crossing the line of scrimmage. Ohhh what a spin move she has! She has a lot of middle linebacker between her and daylight. Now that's a stiff arm. She caught him at the perfect angle then contorted her body to become even lower to the ground and out of reach. Now he's on the ground still grasping to reach Jones. Looking more like someone drowning trying to grab a wave with their hands, trying to tackle the river that was killing them. This is difficult to watch...

As the crowd roared, Traci saw an opening in the secondary. Her feet barely touched the ground. One-by-one the others fell away and she floated on. She felt it. She was a wave. She was the Detroit River.

With one final step across the goal line, history was made. The explosion of exuberant sound was like nothing she had ever imagined. It was as if she could hear beyond the crowd and into the homes across America, as family and friends, gathered together to watch the game, suddenly collectively leapt from their couches, jumping and cheering in disbelief. She removed her helmet and was blinded by tears of joy and humility as she realized that this was not just her moment. It was their moment too, and she was very blessed to be a part of it.

A pride of lions came rushing down the field. Shawn was the first one to reach Traci. He slapped her on the shoulder pads, did an elaborate handshake, chest bumped with her and yelled, "YOU DID IT! YOU DID IT!"

Traci's recently frozen world began spinning once again. As she looked at all the well-wishing faces, she discovered one was missing. Glancing past them, she found Tracy sitting on the sidelines staring at the vacant field.

...

Job walked back into the living room with two ice cream sundaes in hand. He came to an abrupt stop when he saw Disney standing motionless in front of the television with tears streaming down her face. He watched in silence as the voices of John Madden and Al Michael could be heard from the other TV.

Michael asked, *Do you think this celebration is premature?*

Madden answered, *Oh, I don't think so... Was it premature when Neil Armstrong said, That's one small step for man, one giant leap for mankind? We just witnessed another moon landing...*

"Hey," Job said quietly, as he stepped forward, "I made some ice cream sundaes."

Disney whirled around. Flustered and embarrassed, she wiped her tears. "Sorry... I don't know why I'm crying."

"It's alright. I get it." Job handed her a bowl. "That was just the first step. Go on and show them the rest."

Much to Disney's surprise and delight, Job seemed content to sit back on the sofa and let her run the show. Given his bossy nature, she was sure he would want to take over, but he chilled. That's not to say that he didn't offer tidbits of advice. Such as when he said, "I think it is time to put the backups in."

"Not yet," Disney answered, "I want to show them that we are for real... I want to... break the spirits of every team playing in this league."

They had the *crème de la crème* of reasons i.e. they didn't want to be separated as a result of their parents being traded. That said, Job couldn't shake the feeling that they were cheating. Maybe it wasn't a crime, but it damn sure wasn't legal. Whether misdemeanor or felony, it was self-defense, defense of love, their love. Besides, Job and Disney's collective ratiocination indicated that it was the right thing to do. A quarterback five yards over the line of scrimmage, three points down, 10 yards from the endzone with 5 seconds left in the fourth quarter of the Super Bowl had more choices than them. That said, just because someone decided to rob a bank, or in this case the NFL, they didn't have to be rude to the teller/opposing team. And above all enjoy the plunder but not the pillage.

Disney's words indicated one thing, she was enjoying it all. Like watching your loved one say something inappropriate, or do that one thing that embarrasses the shit out of you that everyone else finds funny. You don't want to laugh and encourage them but funny is funny. Plus you don't want to ruin their moment.

And Disney was having a gender and racial caste transcendent moment. Though Job could relate to one, he could only empathize with the other and didn't want to destroy either by lambasting her. Sometimes all you can do is shake your head and laugh, so that's what Job did. Oh and he said, "Woah… sheath your sword, Conan."

"Conan?" Disney inquired without breaking eye contact with the game.

"Conan the Barbarian was—"

"The barbarian?" Disney interrupted.

"Yes, the barbarian," Job said with playful smugness.

Job stared at Disney like an audience of one waiting for a stand-up to deliver the punchline. At the same time Madden began commenting on the real game and Traci's performance.

"*Al, is this a video game?*" John Madden asked with the seriousness of a team doctor at a press conference.

Job and Disney both looked at the television with wide eyes.

"I don't think so, John."

"Good because if this was a game of Madden, I'm pretty sure that Traci deleted his character with that last hit she put on him while he was trying to tackle her!"

Disney laughed as deeply as Job frowned.

"I got Traci out here knockin' mofos out of existence," Disney roared.

"May I continue?" Job volleyed in a humorously pompous tone.

"Yes, you may," Disney said, returning his pompous with a haughty-taught backhand of her own.

"It may be an action movie, John."

"Why'd you say that, Al?"

"Well, says here that Traci is the youngest person to receive a 9th degree black belt in Aikido. An art that teaches one to use force and body weight against an opponent."

"What's the highest rank?" John queried.

"Ten, John. She was scheduled to receive a promotion to 10th dan or degree this summer. It conflicted with practice. So she put it off until next year. Her mom and dad, both black belts, started her at age two!"

"Well, Al, the competition committee never said you couldn't use martial arts. When I was a coach, my philosophy was if the rules don't say you can't do, the rules say you can do it."

"Conan the Barbarian is a warrior in a comic book. In the movie, named—"

"Conan the Barbarian?" Disney said sarcastically.

Job stared at Disney.

"Super surprising title. How do they do it?" Disney asked, with a Mona Lisa smirk.

"Anyway! What was I saying? The book, comic book, is what you would call sword and sorcery. A warrior uses their sword against sorcerers and other warriors. Like tech versus magic. Anyway in the movie a warlord asks Conan "What is best in life?" Conan says, 'To crush your enemies, to see them driven before you, and to hear the lamentations of their women.'"

Disney sucked her teeth as she side-eyed Job and continued her play.

"That's not even sexist," Job joked as he fought back a laugh.

Disney breathed deeply and expelled even more loudly.

"It's much funnier if I don't have to explain it."

"I'm sure it is," Disney tittered.

Job laughed.

"But no that's not it," Disney said seriously.

"Al, you might need to ask that guy for stock and crypto tips."

"Why that, John?"

"Pretty sure Traci knocked him into next week."

"He is pretty shook up, John."

"I've turned Traci into a time machine!" Disney gleefully exclaimed.

Job stopped laughing.

"It's all funny. Even the whole sexist-not-sexist thing. Only a damn fool would think that's not sexist," Disney said without a hint of humor.

Disney twisted her lips in contemplation like a doctor on the verge of a diagnosis.

"Are you a damn fool, Job?"

Job stroked his non-existent goatee.

"Not according to a court of law." Job flashed a proud grin.

Disney rolled her eyes and shook her head.

"You shouldn't do that. Your eyes are going to stay like that," Job jokingly nagged.

"Good! Then when people look at me, they will be scared of me."

"Of course, as that's the goal."

"Especially if there is an eye in my mouth rolling around."

"That's gross," Job said as he twisted his face in disgust.

"Not as gross as eyes on the hands."

Disney flashes her hands at Job palms up.

"How is that connected? And ughhhh!"

Disney laughed until Job found her giggles contagious and joined her. But her own serious thoughts cured her infectious laugh. Job saw her face turn cold and he was inoculated.

"It's just that. Watching or playing this game or whatever it is we are doing got me thinking about how I—we—are trying to use these powers to make this world a better place," Disney pleaded.

If by better place you mean keeping us together, then yes, thought Job.

"Which led me to think about all those who didn't have someone to do that for them. Someone to level the playing field, you know. As I was thinking about that, you brought up Conan and that sexist ass quote, funny sexist ass quote. Which made me think about Sarraounia Mangou," Disney said.

Job's mind meandered. *Maybe I should have went with the Red Sonja quote, from the movie surprisingly named* Rob Sonja. *What did she say? Oh, yeah, "No man may have me, unless he's beaten me in a fair fight." That might work. But Disney is going to ask, "Who did she say it to?"*

Then I have to say this dude, Kalidor, played by the same guy that played Conan. Then explain how non-Conan said, "So, the only man that can have you, is one who's trying to kill you. That's logic." Yeah, that's not going to go over well. Disney will miss the point about the fair fight and get stuck on the whole logic critique.

"Who's Sarraounia? And what does she have to do with Conan?" Job queried.

"She was a female chief, priestess in or abouts Nigeria. When many of the other rulers surrendered to French forces that were trying to colonize the region in the 19th Century. Sarraounia said fuck all y'all and the horses you rode in on! She resisted, mobilized her army and resources to confront the French soldiers. As a result, the French..."

"*Oui oui.*" Job said, with an exaggerated French accent.

"Yes, yes. The French decided that they wanted to

make an example of her. Before they could do this, bish goes to the fortress and attacks!"

"What?!" Job yelled.

"Yes and the French had superior firepower."

"They probably thought it was funny."

"It was until she wasn't an easy go!" Disney

"You know they were hot," Job snickered.

"You probably could cook a full Thanksgiving Dinner—Indigenous People's Day Dinner—on their head. Candied yams, mac and cheese, turkey cooked all the way through. Their heads were so hot. Even a sweet potato pie," Disney cackled.

"With croissants?" Job said through belly laugh breaths.

"If you want that rather than Hawaiian dinner rolls, sure!" Disney shot back.

"Croissants be, yes be so good. Why don't we have any croissant shops?"

"Like donut shops? Why would we?"

"Cause Detroit is French!"

"True true," Disney conceded.

"Is Chicago French?"

"Naw but it was founded by a Black man named Jean Baptiste Point DuSable. Chicago is cold af, probably even colder back then before we had really good winter drip!"

"So Disney, about the domination—"

"Like, you know they were racist. They were definitely in their little white supremacist feelings saying the nerve of this black bitch." Disney shook her head in disgust.

Job nodded.

"So what happened? Did they kill her?" Job inquired.

"They tried buuut she was fearless and used guerrilla tactics. Embarrassed the shit out of them."

"Like you're doing with that guy you just had Traci truck!" Job retorted.

Disney smiled.

"What are you, 15 yards out? Point at the goal line like

you are calling out your shot," Job suggested.

"Did you just think of that?"

"I'm not gonna even hold you up. I want to lie and say yes but it from this old old movie, the Natural. But finish the story."

"She was too much for them. They gave up. And her lands remained free," Disney said with a glint of pride.

"Damn she sounds hard af! Damn Conan!" Job bellowed.

"Right! That's the problem. There are many stories like this of resistance to colonization that we don't hear about. Stories that would inspire people like Traci. Not that she needs it. But inspire women, inspire me. Great stories that should be comic books and films as widely known as Conan. Feel like a lotta white women do themselves a disservice by not using these stories as an example of women getting shit done. But female warriors like the Nzinga Mbandi, the only female leader of the Ashanti, barely get Wikipedia articles."

Job sat down next to Disney.

"Who did you choose?" asked Disney, smiling.

"For my report. Honestly?"

Disney nodded.

"Conan," Job gave a straight-faced reply.

Disney craned her neck and narrowed her eyes so she could properly cast a spell of judgment on Job.

"Pretty sure that look is illegal in 30 states and five countries."

Disney laughed.

"The Empress Dowager Cixi," Job announced.

"Mmmmm, who is that?" asked Disney, with a furrowed brow.

"Well, long story short she was the *de facto* supreme ruler of China for 47 years, from 1861 until her death in 1908. She was a concubine, which is in essence a live-in hoe. She ruled with another concubine," Job said.

"So wait. She went from being a concubine to emperor!?" Disney asked.

"Yes! She was elected as a concubine of the Xianfeng Emperor in her adolescence and gave birth to a son, Zaichun."

"Elected? How the eff do you get elected to be a hoe?" Disney joked.

"I feel you! I'm going to touch on that in the presentation!" Job said with excitement.

"We have to present?"

"Uh yeah!"

"Dang!" Disney mumbled.

"Anyway the Emperor died. So her son became Emperor, and she became the Empress Dowager Cixi. She ousted a group of regents appointed by the late Emperor and assumed regency, which she shared with Empress Dowager Ci'an. Then when her son died, she consolidated control by installing her nephew."

"She could just do that?" Disney asked confused.

"Naw, it's contrary to the traditional rules of succession. Not to mention a woman could not be Emperor so everyone pretended she wasn't really runnin' shit when she was and they knew! Oh and her fellow former concubines."

"Not one but two hoes? Two political geniuses. Do you know how smart you have to be get people that see you as hoes to rule the country?" Disney asked with a giggle.

"Maybe."

"Guess you do, that's why you choose her. Is there a movie about the Empress?" Disney inquired.

"Two. Sort of. And in one of them she is kind of the villain that won't let her nephew rule and clean up corruption. That was in the 70s. The other one was in '89. But nothing with her as the protagonist."

"We have to do this to undo all of this. Traci will have movies."

Traci points to the endzone.

"I think she is calling her shot. Telling the defense she is going to the right side. Wow!" Al Michaels marveled.

"*Yeah, she's directing them to move to the right. They are doing it,*" *John Madden said in astonishment.*

"You know I was joking about the whole point to your shot. You're like the child of Sarraounia and Red Sonja."

Disney crinkled her brow.

"But with a vicious streak."

"Yeah, cause their baby would lack viciousness."

Disney roared with a short burst of laughter that transformed into an ear to ear smile as she warmly gazed at Job, like a bride, moments before she said, 'I do'.

"I know you're worried, Job, but you understand this is more than a game. I know what I'm doing."

Job pursed his lips and nodded.

"Trust me nothing will go wrong. We're in control. We have the power now. Nothing can go wrong."

Job grabbed the controller. He put it down and kissed Disney on the cheek.

"And who is Red Sonja?"

Job imagined the Judgy Mcjudgy look Disney would shoot at him for downloading and retaining all these sexist bytes of data in his RAM. Job buried his face in his hands like a gravedigger forced to dig his own resting place. He kept his face in his grave as he spoke.

"Red Sonja...."

"Speak up, I can't hear you. Why are you covering your face?"

"*Oh wow! I think she knocked him out of his shoes,*" *Al Michaels said.*

"*No, he's still wearing the left one,*" *John Madden said.*

Job stared at Disney.

"That wasn't even vicious!" Disney said as she avoided eye contact with Job.

"It's hard to believe he was trying to tackle her. She delivered a ferocious hit!"

"Seeeee!"

Job voluntarily stepped back into the grave he made with his hand.

"Red Sonja...like you a warrior...with a vicious streak?"

...

Vicious but not entirely heartless. In the end, the Vikings scored seven to the Lions' seventy-seven. Disney joined Job on the sofa just in time to watch the post-game interviews. Josina Anderson was the lucky reporter to grab this week's golden girls for interviews.

When Branson walked past the trio, Disney pointed excitedly to the screen. "Oh look, there's Dad."

"If he ever gave interviews, he would get more endorsements," Job said.

Disney waved her hand in dismissal. "You know how he is… all business, no celebrity."

Job considered his father. Shawn was more fifty/fifty. On the field he was all business, but given the opportunity he could ham it up with the best of them. "Must be nice."

Billie, did you expect such an impressive victory in your inaugural game as a head coach? Josina asked.

Yes.

Josina seemed taken aback by Billie's gruff, concise response. As she fumbled for her next question, Shawn ran towards them and hoisted Traci on his shoulders.

Job pointed to the screen. Shaking his head and laughing, he said, "See what I mean."

Josina looked up at Traci, perched on Shawn's shoulders, and jumped at the opportunity to capture the moment on screen, *Coming into this game there was so much talk of whether or not your body could take the punishment. After running for over 500 yards, how do you feel?*

Traci looked straight at the camera with a wide smile. *I feel like I could run another 500 yards. The hits hurt, but honestly, it would hurt more if I were denied the opportunity to be hit.*

Shawn pointed to someone off screen and then yelled out, *Tracy, get over here and show your woman some love.*

An awkward pause followed. Disney peeled her eyes from the screen and looked over at Job. "Why isn't he coming over?"

In unison, Job, and Shawn on the TV screen, shrugged. Shawn carried Traci to the locker room, leaving Josina alone with Billie. Josina looked back at Billie with a nervous smile.

Your husband must be so proud. Where is Stan?

Stan is in Knoxville with his team. Thank you. Billie ended the interview with a nod and joined her team in the locker room. She placed her hand on the door but it opened for her.

"Coach!" Traci said as she stepped through.

Billie brandished a full smile.

"How are you feeling?" Billie queried.

"My hamstring is a little sore but—"

"Are you injured or you hurt?"

"Hell, Coach, at this point in the season, I'm probably hurt!"

Billie and Traci both laughed.

"Where are you headed?"

"To the casino with my girls to celebrate."

Billie guided Traci out of the doorway by placing her hands on her shoulders. She locked eyes with Traci, and teared up.

"Coach? You good?" Traci asked with concern.

Billie didn't cry. Or at least she never called it that. When people asked if she was crying, she always had some snappy retort. But no snappy retort could put a lid on the brewing pot of feelings wafting from her heart to her peepers. An aroma stronger than yellow onions. An aroma almost as strong as the smell of victory wafting from the locker room. Way better than the stink of defeat that she expected to inhale after her coaching debut.

So was she good? At this moment in the fourth dimension, otherwise known as time, Billie was so beyond good. And how far beyond depended upon who was asking. Depended upon with whom she was sharing the fourth dimension. As she eyed Traci, Billie's heart wondered. In any dimension, the heart feels faster than the mind thinks. Billie felt the magnitude of this moment faster than her mind could process it because in football, Latif Test and Bechdel-Walle moments did not occur.

The Latif Test is a measure of the adequacy of racial diversity and representation in fiction. Not to be confused with the Bechdel-Wallace Test, which is a measure of the representation of women in fiction. Fun fact: technically the Latif Test should be called the Latif-Latif Test as it was created by two sisters, Nadia Latif and Leila Latif.

If this were a movie, they both would be two named characters, Traci and Billie. Check. They could have dialogue, supportive dialogue if Billie could open her damn mouth to speak. So check. They were not romantically involved with one another. They were both women. Check. Their conversation concerned each of their respective performances, i.e. they were not talking about a man. And though they were both Black, neither was magic i.e. neither was a wise, folksy black character with magical forces or spiritual insight to help white characters along their hero's journey.

Billie expected that she would coach in the NFL. But never had she expected that her star player would be a Black woman playing a position that she was never allowed to even try out for. But those passing grades could change depending on to which Traci she was speaking. If Billie was speaking to Traci, the woman standing in front of her that was young enough to be her child, Billie wanted to ask if she was ok. If it was Traci the running back, her running back, Billie wanted to tell her how proud she was. If it was Traci the woman that had broken barriers, she wanted to warn her about all the dangers the 3rd rock from the sun would bring her way in the coming days. The latter would force Billie to give counsel that would raise subjects that had always been discussed in movies by two Black women like them. Today she did not want to rain on Traci. Periodt. Billie wanted to thank each and every one of them for making her look like a Tony Dungy. The only acceptable rain, in Billi's eyes, figuratively and literally would be a storm of tears.

"You look like you are about to cry," Traci said. Sounding more like she was asking a question than making a statement of fact.

"No, just lubricating my eyes," Billie responded.

"Yeah, well, I see a mixture of water, lipids, enzymes, glucose, and sodium streaming down your face."

Billie laughed as the non-tears pranced down her face.

"I'm so proud of you!" Billie said, as she tried to capture each tear before it skipped.

"Aww thank you Coach! You came up with the perfect game plan!"

A hug is usually initiated by holding out one's arms and waiting for the other person's response. Traci reached out and drew her hand back several times like a gif.

"Are you having a stroke?"

Traci roared with laughter.

"Oh, you want to hug! Come here!" Billie said, like she was Scorpion from Mortal Kombat. Fortunately, this was not followed by an ominous voice saying finish her. Instead it was followed by the delivery of something family therapist Virginia Satir once said humans require. We need 4 per day for survival. We need 8 per day for maintenance and we need 12 hugs a day for growth. A hug doesn't become intimate or cause someone to release oxytocin, the bonding hormone, until it reaches over 20 seconds. The embrace bonds the two participants and fires up the brain's trust circuitry, leading to the comforting stage. Sadly, few hugs, whether they be Latif-Latif or Bechdel-Wallace in nature, last long enough to reach the comforting stage.

Billie and Traci embraced. It was the first hug in weeks for both of them. It lasted 30 seconds.

"When it comes to sports, women are big targets for abuse because the resentment is two-fold. Some resent us for our confidence and beliefs. But there also is an added resentment because we are supposedly infiltrating a space that has been decidedly male."
~Jamelle Hill, Sport Journalist, Activist, and Host

Well, everyone is slurping the Lions. If I have to be the lone voice of dissent then so be it. The Lions haven't played anyone of merit. Talk to me after Green Bay. Until then, I won't even entertain the phrase 'Super Bowl bound'. Instead, I quote the great Jim Mora, "Playoffs, playoffs, Are you kidding me!" I will wear pink tights if the Lions make the playoffs.

Disney snickered at Bob Ryan, a reporter from Boston, on SportsCenter.

I agree, all this talk of the Lions is premature… my bet is not on the Lionesses… Bob's counterpart retorted.

Hey now… Lisa Salters, the lone female reporter interjected… *those Lionesses are winning games. And while Traci has been accused of PED use, there is zero evidence of this beyond her superior performance. A fact that the trifecta, consisting of owner, coach, and player will likely address in their first unified press conference. Oh, I hear that they are set to begin. Let's listen in to what they have to say…*

…

Cleo sat in the middle of a podium, sandwiched between Billie and Traci. Of the three, Cleo felt the least prepared to face the media barrage, but it was a necessary evil. She needed to counter the rumors that had started floating around after last week's unprecedented victory, which had broken the longstanding record set by Washington in 1966. Cleo scanned the room for mirrors. She was rocking her first ever adult outfit, a pantsuit. She wanted to see it.

Despite a growling nervous stomach, a warm glow radiated in her heart as these pieces of fabric made her feel competent for the first time in her adult life. She took one final sip of water, hoping to wash away the nervous crackle that tickled her throat, and prepared to read the official statement of the Lions' organization that had been drafted by their legal department.

"Thank you all for coming today. Over the past couple of days the Lions have been subjected to malicious rumors and allegations, which deeply offend me both as a team owner and a woman. When they said a woman would never play as a running back, we proved them wrong. When they said we would never win, we proved them wrong. Now, the woman who has shattered the glass stadium has been falsely accused of using illegal and banned substances. The Lions organization has never tolerated doping, and our players are subjected to random drug testing, just like all players in the league. At the beginning of the season, Traci Jones tested negative for all banned substances. The demands that she be retested are unfair, unjust, and unprincipled.

"The source of Jones' talent would not be questioned if she were a man. Having said this, Traci Jones graciously volunteered to retest—on the spot—to end these distracting rumors. As we fully expected, the results have come back negative. We are willing to take questions now."

Hands flew up and voices howled. Most of them seemed to be yelling Traci's name.

"Ms. Jones, we are going into week four undefeated, how does that feel?"

Traci leaned forward with a wide smile. "In one word—amazing."

"Traci, you and your fiancé, Tracy Gideon, have been regulars in the Detroit nightlife scene, but lately you have been conspicuously absent. Is your newfound success putting pressure on your relationship?"

Before she could answer, Billie leaned into her mic, and said, "Next question."

The group of reporters started chuckling when one claimed that Billie had just thrown a flag on that question. Traci glanced down the table at Billie with a silent *Thank you* in her eyes.

"Billie, do you think being a woman has made the role of head coach more challenging?"

"No," Billie answered in her typical gruff fashion, which the press was beginning to expect.

"Billie, any thoughts about tomorrow's game?"

"Yes… of winning."

"Cleo, who are you wearing?"

"Are you kidding me?" Billie grumbled. "This is an NFL press conference, not the Golden goddamn Globes. And from here on out call me Coach f******* Wall and her Ms. f****** White!"

Billie, Charlie, and Traci rose to their feet to exit. As they neared the exit, Billie turned around, grabbed the mic and with a smile said to the room, "God bless."

•••

Job reached for the remote and turned off the TV. "We have some work to do."

Disney flipped her wrist at him. "What are you talking about?"

"I changed the settings. We can play anytime and the game will follow our game."

Disney sighed as she took the remote from his hand. "Oh."

"What's your problem?"

With a grumpy shrug, she settled into the sofa cushions. "I don't know. I guess I'm just thinking about the press conference and the cheating rumors."

Job waved his hand in dismissal and then turned on the PlayStation. "We both know those aren't true."

She wasn't convinced. "Aren't they? Maybe they aren't doping, but they are winning because we are playing the game for them. Now, Traci is the first female running back, Billie the first female coach in the NFL, and Cleo..."

"Am I in an episode of *Black Mirror*? Didn't I say that?"

"Why you bringin' up old shit?"

"Old? Has it even been a month?"

"Nobody needs all that truth, Job!" Disney said, as she swallowed a laugh.

Job's lips puckered in defiance. "I can't with you. What was I about to say? Yeah, that just isn't true. Cleo started playing the game before we did. She was the one that chose Billie and Billie moved Traci. That was all on *them*. Plus we don't know what this game does for sure. It could technically just give them confidence. Keep in mind, Traci played running back in high school and returned to it in college. She is so small, 5'4 , 5'7, it's like the defense loses her. Sometimes it's like finding a needle in a haystack. But just when you think you have it, the needle stabs you in the hand, you drop it, and it scores a touchdown."

Disney nodded in agreement. Job thought about quitting while he was ahead. It would be like kicking a field goal. Three points was three points. But he was on the goal line and if he punched it in, he would never have to have this conversation again. Seven was definitely more than three. "Now would she have run for the most yards ever in a single game? Ehhhhhh... maybe?"

Disney's vertical yes changed into a horizontal no faster than a wide receiver on a ten day contract running a slant route.

"Yeah right! But confidence… that's still help, Job. That's a competitive advantage. They are still cheating in some way, only they don't know it. Doesn't that bother you, even a little bit?"

Job carefully considered her question for a moment. "Not really. You were the one who wanted Traci "The River" Jones."

"I know," Disney hissed. "But I really wanted her to be able to do it on her own."

"You don't know that she can't," Job challenged. "We did what we had to do, and it opened up possibilities that had been previously closed, but neither of us knows if Traci could or couldn't do it on her own. She was scoring touchdowns in high school, delivering hits in college, and kicking that ball on a pro level way before we got this PlayStation. And as far as Billie is concerned, my dad said that everyone in the league knows that her husband, what's his name, has been holding her back for years."

"Hmmpt."

Job closed his eyes and took a deep breath. The convincing of the Disney would require a lot more time and energy.

...

Job played the game with his usual gusto. Today they were playing Green Bay, and he knew how important this game was. Disney remained uncharacteristically quiet. He knew this was really bothering her, but there wasn't anything they could do about it… not now at least. If they stopped playing, they risked everything going back to the way it was before. And if they did that, the glass stadium would be super-glued shut with a NASA strength adhesive. It would be years before another NFL team took a chance on a female player. Sometimes you play to win the game. Sometimes you play because failure is no longer an option. Trailblazers are not allowed to fail.

Thankfully, he had something in his pocket that might lift her spirits. Once they defeated Green Bay sixty-five to twenty, Job pulled out the tickets his father had given him.

"What's that?" Disney asked.

"My dad told Cleo about how much we love football, and she invited us to sit in her box for tomorrow's game."

"Arghhh," Disney yelled.

Startled, the controller slipped between his fingers and dropped to the floor. "*What*?!?"

"What do you mean '*What*'? I'm obviously happy that we are going to watch the game in the owner's box!" Disney barked in the unhappiest of tones.

Job's left brow crept up like Sherlock Holmes. He concluded that it must be time to play mind reader. "Obviously... happy and *conflicted*?" his voice rose in question.

"#ConflictedAF," Disney said while shaking her head.

They both burst into laughter.

"Pro football is like nuclear warfare. There are no winners, only survivors."
~Frank Gifford, Defensive Back, Running Back, New York Giants

On the rare occasions Cleo White had thought about football while growing up, she had always believed it to be a brutal sport. She had never in her life expected that one day she would find herself on the receiving end of that brutality. In the span of a few months, she had gone from an unknown to a hashtag that was more often than not a dumping ground for her many fashion *faux pas*. Commentators, reporters, fashion bloggers, and armchair trolls had ripped her to shreds for everything from the clothes she wore to the style of her hair to the type of phone she carried.

The latest debacle was a series of viral subtweets, comments, memes, and gifs, where she found herself being attacked by critics from across the globe because she had worn an ill-fitting pantsuit from Wal-Mart during her first press conference. In her defense, power clothes always made her feel like a flight attendant, and she typically erred on the side of comfort, even in the IG post on her private account with 10 followers that she thought were her friends. Just like that, the warm glow she felt by presenting herself like a competent adult was snuffed out by a hoard of mean-spirited people, who clearly had too much time on their hands.

Billie was not entirely unsympathetic. In her typical fashion, Billie told her that she had two options: either ignore them or fight back. Then again, Billie had bigger issues to deal with at the moment, and the miracles she pulled out of her hat every Sunday were the very least of them. As Billie was staunchly private and more than a little intimidating, Cleo would never dream of prying into her personal affairs, but she was confident that Billie had to be devastated. It was absolutely mind-blowing that Stan had yet to attend a single game.

The blood-thirsty sharks that swam amongst real reporters never failed to mention his absence, yet Billie always offered the same unemotional excuse. They were more like blood-thirsty dolphin sharks mixed as they followed the story arc build you up, then tore you down, only to build you back up. Sometimes during that in-between time, you could starve waiting for that build back up. However there was one exception: winning. If you won, they were way more dolphins than sharks, suddenly willing to guide sailors through all types of stormy sport seas.

In the meantime, the crux of Billie's argument was always that he was simply too busy. Too busy to show even a morsel of support for his wife that spent over thirty years supporting him. Cleo was furious on Billie's behalf. Of course, Billie would never give any credence to the press's war of spouses, but, if she did, Billie would undoubtedly be the victor. As far as Cleo could decipher, Billie was only interested in winning on the field, and what happened off the field was no one else's damn business.

It was an unspoken policy that Billie shared with the players, and with good reason. All the unprecedented changes had sparked a media firestorm. Seemingly overnight, they had slipped past the narrow confines of football and had been tossed like sheep to the wolves of the general public, who were not satisfied until every detail was brought to light. Move over Meghan Markle and Prince Harry! Royalty was old news. The sharks now fed off the blood of Lions, and they wanted EVERYTHING. Who the Lions dated? What clothes did they wear? What music did they listen to? No details of the team's private lives belonged to them anymore. Speculations of the "Tracies" engagement were now regular features on entertainment segments. A few of the players even said that paparazzi were being spotted at their children's schools.

Cleo occasionally found herself copy-pasting foreign tweets into Google Translate, curious what the rest of the world was saying. What looked so eloquent in French roughly translated to '...sloppy woman...' Though minor in the grand scheme of things, these translated comments still stung. Then there was the bargaining that Cleo would do with herself after the translation spat through. Maybe it was wrong? She knew that Google Translate sometimes made mistakes, but this seemed particularly close to home for an inaccurate translation. Plus, did the French even like football? The French word for football literally translated to mean soccer, distinct from 'le football Américain '. Well, sort of. When you type in football in the French box on Google Translate, the English translation is still soccer.

Cleo quickly grew tired of the media shots at her fashion sense, but she knew it could be much worse. At least her relationship was not under the microscope. Of course, this was mostly because her boyfriend was imaginary. Besides, if Stan and Tracy were anything to go by, at this stage in her life this was probably for the best. She was also grateful that creepers were not hiding in the bushes at her children's school, because they too were imaginary—the children, that is. Unfortunately, the creepers were all too real. This made Cleo reconsider Billie's sage advice. Her options were dwindling down to one. If, as the leader and owner, she did not fight back, who would?

"Excuse me, Cleo White?" The statement pulled her away from her meanderings about life under scrutiny of the public eye. She was expecting guests. Shawn Lamb had mentioned to her, earlier this week, that his son and his son's friend were huge fans of the game. It gave her a perfect excuse to watch the game with someone besides the usual suits, and this delighted her. She stood up from her seat and turned around to face her guests as they entered the owner's box.

Teenagers? Why hadn't Shawn mentioned that they were teenagers? In her mind, she had envisioned something a little more cute and sociable—the kinds of kids who were still thrilled by Happy Meal toys and could be pacified with an iPad. Teenagers were the worst. Cleo vividly remembered that stage of her life, best described as tumultuous. She had been rude, surly, and basically thought all adults were idiots. Though as her mind flashed back to the Tweets from France, it occurred to her that her teen years were really only slightly more tumultuous than her current life.

"Hello, you must be Job and Disney," Cleo said, sounding even to her own ears, overly cheerful.

Just a few moments into their visit, Cleo discovered, much to her surprise and relief, that Job and Disney were nothing like the teen that she had once been. Disney was a bubble of happiness, and Job was reserved but he possessed a courteousness that seemed well beyond his years. They were both certainly easier to talk to than the rest of the half-dozen or so people in the box, most of whom were middle-aged billionaires along with their trophy wives, maybe also a few trophy husbands and partners... but very few. It had the makings of a perfect Sunday Funday until a small group of men were paraded into the box and then directed to stand in the front as if they were on display.

Cleo walked forward and addressed the office intern. "Excuse me? Can you please tell me what is going on?"

"Miss White, these are the homeless people you ordered," he explained.

Horrified, Cleo glanced at the children whose natural curiosity had prompted them to follow her. "I..." she gasped. "I...

never ordered homeless people. As part of our ongoing community outreach, we have given an open invitation to many of the local shelters," she explained, trying to remain calm. Then with as much tact as she could muster, Cleo whispered the obvious, "Why… are they dressed like that?"

"Tip said to make them look presentable… only not too presentable," the intern winked.

As Cleo looked at the men who were all wearing shirts at least three sizes too small, which appeared extremely uncomfortable, and pants five sizes too large, Tip sauntered over.

"It would defeat the purpose otherwise," Tip said.

"Just once…" Cleo spat, "…it would be nice if you remembered that you are a human and not a soulless asshole."

Instantly, Cleo regretted her choice of words and turned back to the kids. Before she could offer an apology, Cleo discovered that Job had already stripped off his jersey. Now dressed in a plain white T-shirt and jeans, he handed the jersey to a man whose given shirt was so tight that he could not move his arms.

"Go on, take it," Job prompted. "And keep it. No worries, bruh."

Cleo instructed the intern to find the gentlemen real clothes to wear. Contrary to Tip's notions of making the men puppets on display, Cleo tried her best to reassure them that they were here to simply enjoy themselves. Afterwards, she sat down with Job and Disney.

Still mortified, she leaned over and whispered, "I'm sorry you had to see that."

Job laughed it off. "We are football brats. Trust me, we've both heard worse… in our homes."

"That… and Tip. How tone deaf can one person be? Not everyone in the organization shares his heartless attitude," Cleo said.

Disney flashed a blindingly bright smile. "I know."

"So tell me, what did I miss?" Cleo asked.

"The kicker kicked the ball out of bounds on the kick off," Disney said.

"Now the other team has been penalized forty yards," Job added.

"The middle linebacker is spying the quarterback," Disney said.

Cleo seemed to be following along until the last part so Job explained, "He's spying my dad. Spying means watching to see if he will run."

With their excellent tutoring, Cleo finally started to grasp the game. For the first time, she understood what Al Michaels was talking about when she heard him on the television screen say, *"Well, let's see what they do on 3rd and forty. Not that it matters with this score, but I expect that they will down it and run the clock out."*

Cleo leaned forward in her seat and watched as Shawn snapped the ball.

"It's a blitz," Disney yelled out.

Engrossed in the game, Cleo failed to see the cautious glance Job shot in Disney's direction. Instead, Cleo's eyes were glued to the field below. Her hands covered her mouth when Traci was smashed by two linemen. Then in a panic, Shawn crossed the line of scrimmage. He tucked the ball and juked two linemen so hard that they both appeared to have sprained their ankles, yet hobbled after him all the same.

He should be stopped at the forty by the safety well short of the first down... Madden predicted.

BUT NO! Cleo's hands rose from her mouth and stayed poised in the air above her head. Instead of sliding, Shawn shot towards them. The safeties attempted to sandwich him, but he leapt over one like a frog and then crashed into the other. Midair, Shawn whirled around like an airplane and somehow miraculously landed on his feet.

As Shawn skipped into the end zone, Madden said, *"I'm speechless...totally without words. I have seen it all. I feel like I'm watching a human video game."*

"They don't keep score at the press conference but when it's over we all know who won and who lost it."
~Demetrius Jones, Sports and Entertainment Attorney, Author

"This isn't my first rodeo, Tip," Cleo spat, as Tip blocked her way to the press room.

"Yeah," Tip scoffed, "it's technically your second. All I am trying to say is you don't have to do this. Maybe if you jumped down from your hashtag "Me Two Three Four" High Horse, you might be able to savor the feeling of victory."

Ignoring him, Cleo slipped past him.

"You're making a big mistake, Cleo," Tip called out after her.

Cleo whirled around on her heels. The sudden movement in her new pair of Amina Abdul Jillil's high high heels, which she was unaccustomed to wearing, caused her ankles to wobble, yet somehow she managed to recover with a gracious flair.

"My mistakes have sold more tickets and merch than your so called successes. Sorry, not sorry, Tip, but I got to go with the gut on this."

Cleo passed Billie on her way to the podium. Out of the view of the camera's all-seeing eye, Billie whispered, "Go get them."

Cleo maintained her poise and answered question after question in a clear, direct style. This was a little trick she had picked up by watching Billie. Cleo had changed. Not sure of the exact moment, but somewhere amidst the encounters with the media, Billie, the players, Job, Disney, and almost every other aspect of this new life, it had finally changed her into something different. Unbeknownst to her spectators, under her cool façade was the heart of a vicious hunter waiting for the first opportunity to strike. She felt like a lion.

"Allie, isn't it?" Cleo asked, as she pointed towards one of the reporters.

"Yes... Cleo, first of all, congratulations. The real question everyone wants to know: who are you wearing?"

Cleo tucked her head to hide her smirk, which was misinterpreted as a sign of frustration and an omen of an impending tongue-lashing regarding the ridiculous double-standards that were still forced upon women in a *so-called* modern society.

"Fair question," Cleo admitted in a clipped but amiable tone, as she lifted her eyes to the crowd, "to be honest, there were a few miscalculations on my part, which I will own. As we all know, when two or more white women are gathered, and Stevie Nicks' *Landslide*, Beyoncé's *Formation*, or SZA's *Weekend* are all played within seconds of each other, women's menstrual cycles will sync. And honestly, if Elon Musk is so determined to earn his place in the Hall of Greatness, he could start by inventing a fabric that could withstand post-Brazilian stubble... so in the end, I had to pull out a second-string pair of Hanes Her Way. The elastic is warped and the front panel shoddy, but I made it work..." Cleo paused as she looked across their speechless faces.

"Any other questions? Pre/post period bra-size? Body fat ratio? Latest crush? No? Nothing? Sorry, I must have confused you with the unprofessional members of the press who insist on questioning both me and my players about everything except what we are actually doing, which is winning games and making history," she concluded.

...

Stripped out of her armor, Traci sat alone in her street clothes in a closet-sized space that was the newly designated women's locker room. She dreamed of the day when it would hold more than one locker and a single shower stall that reminded her of middle school with its yellow tiles. She was not ready to face the onslaught just yet, but she did not want to be alone either. She never dreamed her life could change so fast, and the all-or-nothingness was playing with her head. Either she was surrounded by people screaming her name and begging for pictures and autographs or she was completely alone. Toying with the five-carat diamond engagement ring, she slipped it on and off her finger.

The thing the press did not understand was that once she got past her first game jitters, the fear of running into a pack of men, most of whom were double or even triple her size, whose entire goal was to squish her flatter than an iPhone, was nothing. At least, not compared to the heartbreak of going home alone every night.

It was over. Traci knew deep in her soul that it was over. In the past couple of months, Tracy had only spoken a few perfunctory words. Still, every night she hoped and prayed that something would come his way. Tracy was a proud man. Playing second fiddle to his woman just was not part of his DNA. Still that was not an excuse for his behavior last night. Caught by the local news, Tracy had been spotted at a local sports bar playing what Traci had unaffectionate named, "King Shit of Turd Mountain" i.e King Shit or Tracy was surrounded by football groupies, barely legal, with a girl sitting on his lap. *Hmmm,* Traci's mind processed the scene, Tracy on the news dry humping with some random *...the random was a really cute girl, and at least the random was Black... at least Tracy wasn't a total cliché i.e. an extremely successful Black guy with a white girl waitress/IG model who, if she was a Black waitress/IG model, he* *wouldn't give a second look. Ugh! Silly thoughts that mean the world and nothing at all.*

As much as Traci wanted to rip through the screen, another part of her, the foolish half of her heart, was relieved to see the story had only made the local news. She almost felt sorry for Tracy, because he was now so insignificant that The Shade Room, Bossip, and Baller Alert, all failed to pick up the juicy morsel of gossip. Not so much as a chirp on Black Twitter or whisper on TMZ Sports.

Fighting back the tears, Traci hoisted herself off the bench and slowly made the move towards the men's locker room. As much as it broke her heart, Tracy needed to be reminded who he had publicly humiliated. As soon as she stepped into the men's locker room, all cameras, players and personnel eyes pivoted in her direction. With the world watching, she walked straight towards Tracy who was sitting alone at his locker, sulking in the back corner.

"Here, take it. I don't want it anymore," Traci announced, as she held the engagement ring in her hand.

The scowl deepened on his face as Tracy looked past her and straight into the twenty plus cameras and eyes that were pointed in his direction. He stood up and began swiping his hands across his thighs.

"Nah," he denied. "Save it for your next soul mate."

...

Billie gave Stan a play-by-play of the game, and he pretended that he had not watched it. It was the only shred left he had of his pride... that and pretending that he did not miss her. The truth was that ever since she had moved to Detroit, nothing felt right. Food did not taste good. The house was too quiet. Practices felt uninspiring. His head felt fuzzy during the games. Just about the only thing he looked forward to anymore was Sundays, and even then, he found himself watching the game less-and-less, yet sitting on the edge of his chair more-and-more whenever he caught a glimpse of his wife. Trying to play coy, Stan ended the call with Billie.

Before he had a chance to further bemoan his existence, his phone rang again. This time it was Tip.

"Stan here."

"Stan, how's it going?" Tip asked.

"Just as you could imagine," Stan answered. Then again, Tip had been married three times. None of his marriages had lasted more than a few years, so maybe he couldn't imagine. "If you are calling to tell me the plan isn't going so well, I already figured that out."

"I never pegged you as a quitter," Tip murmured. "Rest assured, I just discovered our ace in the hole."

Stan sighed as he ran his hand over the top of his head. It was not until Billie had left him that he had noticed how sparse his hairline had gotten. Just about the same time, he noticed all the deep crevasses that were beginning to crisscross his face. In fact, one morning, about a week after Billie had left, as he was looking in the mirror getting ready to shave, Stan had realized that he had grown into an old man. Far too old to start over.

"Look, Tip, I've had some time to think this over, and I won't be a part of anything that could damage Billie's reputation. She's earned it fair and square, whether either of us like it or not," Stan answered.

"Stan…" Tip chuckled. "The only one who will ruin Billie's reputation is Billie. All you need to do is stay sharp and ready."

…

The following Monday, Tip asked Branson to stop by his office after practice. Branson did not have a good feeling about either Tip or his request, but he was not in the position to deny him.

The team played at Ford Field in downtown Detroit. But the Lions' headquarters and practice facilities were located in Allen Park, a collection of communities known as Downriver. Fun fact, Allen Park is home to the Uniroyal Giant

Tire, the largest non-production tire scale model ever built, and one of the world's largest roadside attractions. It was originally a Ferris wheel at the 1964 New York World's Fair, and was moved to Allen Park in 1966.

Set on 22.7 acres at the Southfield Freeway and Rotunda Drive, the Lions' facility consisted of a high indoor practice field, staff offices, broadcast studio, theatre, weight room, locker rooms, rehab facilities, kitchen and dining area, players' lounge, and an observation area for the indoor field. Tip's office was near the observation area, probably so he could spy on every damn body. Branson sauntered over to Tip's office after visiting the locker room for a shower.

Branson took his seat and figured that although he couldn't smell it, some type of BS would soon make its appearance and overpower the smell of jasmine radiating from the Vangogh360 Cold-fusion scent diffuser working hard in the corner. At first, Tip tried to play it smooth like they were old buddies, which they most definitely were not. Tip even asked about Debbie and Disney. Branson knew it was a play. Tip didn't give a flying flip about Branson's wife and child. Everyone knew the only person Tip cared about was Tip.

After a few minutes of pretending to be a family man, Tip shifted gears, revealing his true purpose.

"Branson, I have the deepest respect for you and your opinion. I'm not alone. Others have come and gone, but you've stayed the course. You are the silent soul of this organization. It's because of this, that I need to ask you a very important question. And I need your honesty. What are your true feelings about Billie and Traci?"

Here cometh the bullshit. Branson shifted in his seat. "They both work real hard."

Tip nodded and cast a studious glance around his office. He seemed to fully respect Branson's opinion. But then a questioning frown puckered his lips. "And... you aren't bothered in the least that they are women?"

"On the field, I don't have a lot of time to think about it."

Tip leaned back in his chair and propped his feet on his desk. "Certainly, at the moment, the Lions are the media's darlings despite Cleo's best efforts to make it otherwise... but my gut feeling is that the bubble will burst. Football is a man's sport, and not just any man... manly men. Once all these fly-by-nights find their next big thing, that is who will be left. Our true fans. Let's face it, men like that don't want to see women in the locker rooms. Period."

Branson's mouth slammed shut and he refused to look in Tip's direction.

"I meant what I said. I do have the deepest respect for you Branson, and for that reason alone, I have squelched details of your past that are better left private. But... the day is coming where it might be out of my hands. My gut feeling is that all this media attention isn't going away until we find a way to deal with the problem. Don't you agree?"

The men stared at one another for a year-long minute. Then Branson looked down at the floor and thought, "Damn, it stinks in here."

"Life is TEN percent what happens to you, and NINETY percent how you respond to it."
~Lou Holtz, Head Coach, Notre Dame

"I think maybe we should chill out," Disney said when Job handed her the controller.

"What are you talking about?"

Job wouldn't understand. He didn't pay much mind to something as simplistic as intuition. "I don't know. I've just got a bad feeling."

"Maybe it's just mid-season jitters. You will feel better if we break a hundred," Job answered.

Disney crossed her arms over her chest in defiance. "No. We need to lose a game. This is getting out of control. I know you think we are playing the game, but maybe the game is playing us. If we keep going how we are going, do you know whose record we are about to break? For one, the Dolphins' undefeated season, for two the single season rushing record, for three passing record, for four, yes, I know that sounds weird, for five, yes I know that sounds weirder, for six fewest points allowed, for seven most passing touchdowns, for eight rushing downs, for nine fumbles caused and recovered, and for ten most interceptions. So basically the whole record book!"

Although it was hard to imagine, Disney could be a force to be reckoned with when her mind was set. Job waved his hand in surrender. "Okay. I understand. I promise we will lose the last game before the Super Bowl."

"*Boy*, what are you not understanding?" Disney rolled her eyes in frustration. "No... no we shouldn't be going to the Super Bowl! I thought you just wanted to stay here. We've done that already."

Job set down his controller and reached for her hand. "Disney, you've got to understand what this team is about. They have *never* won a Super Bowl. I mean like for real never. They won championships, but it's like, once they changed the name of the big game to Super Bowl, they forgot how to win."

Disney pulled her hand free. She didn't want to have to come out and say it. Playing this game was changing Job, and not for the better. "Maybe you forgot how to lose? Or at least the difference between right and wrong?"

"What harm can it do? The teams that are supposed to be there will be there next year," Job countered.

"Well, *Mr. Scientist,* have you ever heard of the butterfly effect?"

Job grunted and shook his head in disbelief, which told her that he knew exactly where she was going with this argument. Disney expected to be countered with a half dozen reasons why that wouldn't apply to their situation but instead she got none. "Just one... okay."

Job's lack of response frightened her because his silence admitted that he realized there could be unforeseen consequences. Disney expelled a long suffering sigh. She could not shake the feeling that something was about to go wrong. It was just like her mom was fond of saying: if it seems too good to be true then it probably is. Throughout Job's game, her eyes drifted to the other television in the room. The camera panned to the sideline where Billie was laughing with Tip. Disney's lips sneered in disgust as she wondered what they were discussing.

...

"Coach," Tracy yelled as he jogged towards Billie and Tip, "I forgot my cup. I need to go back to the locker room."

"We're up by thirty... you're not going back in. Don't worry about it," Billie answered.

As soon as Billie turned away, Tracy's steely eyes narrowed with loathing and a sneer curled his lip. He was a football player damnit, not some sort of sideshow puppet in a female dynasty. If Billie wanted to be a matriarch, then she should take up with a herd of elephants. Lions ran this pride. Tracy studied the defense as they took formation. They are about to blitz. *Perfect.* Tracy glanced at Branson and tapped his head with both fists. Branson nodded silently.

The offense was once again set and ready. The ball was snapped. Tracy was right, it was a blitz. Shawn handed the ball to Traci. Traci followed behind Branson. A DE rushed towards them. Branson prepared to block the defensive end, but in the final second, he let him slip past.

Traci did not see the defensive end and his force blindsided her! One second her feet were on the ground and the next second they were not. She caught a glimpse of her helmet as it flew off her head. Still holding the ball, she tried to get up but crumbled and fell back to the ground. She grasped her ankle, and Shawn dove to her side. Billie pulled Shawn back to make room for the training staff. Billie watched in silence as there was no need to ask Traci if she was injured or hurt. A stadium filled with over 65,000 people and all that could be heard was the howl of one injured lion.

...

"What!?" Job shouted. "Your dad missed the block on purpose!"

"Job, why would he do that?" Disney cried defensively. "It doesn't make sense...my dad would never do that!"

"It doesn't have to make sense. He did it. I saw it. LOOK," Job exclaimed as he grabbed the remote and clicked rewind. After the replay, he looked over at Disney and said, "See, see, he just stopped!"

Disney's mouth gaped open with disbelief as she slowly walked towards the television screen. Her hands moved to cover her mouth. A whisper slipped past the fingers. "No."

Once again in live time, she watched as Shawn screamed at her father. She could not hear what he was saying but his animated motions were a sign language of their own. Branson pointed to someone off screen.

In the midst of the chaos, Madden announced, *Well folks… it appears we are playing the blame game now.*

The camera followed Shawn as he raced across the field. Tip turned around and saw Shawn rushing forward with his head tucked low. He stepped out of the way just in time, but Tracy was not so lucky. Seconds later, Tracy was on the ground. Shawn was sitting on top of him with his fist drawn back.

Billie rushed forward and grabbed Shawn's fist before he could plow it into Tracy's face. *"Have you lost your mind?"*

Tracy remained curled in a ball with his hands covering his face.

"She will be fine… she has on pads." Tracy said venomously.

Billie hauled both of them off the ground. "We'll discuss this later… *off camera.*"

…

Tears rolled down Disney's cheeks as she continued to watch everything unfolding, half in disbelief. Disney's legs felt weak. Her heart sank as her sense of self drained from her body. It's a vampiric coming of age experience when you first learn that your Dad can make mistakes. An experience that should have occurred over the time that it took for her to go from a teenager to a 20-year-old. Instead it happened all at once, and her world crumbled under the weight of that moment.

The twins helped Traci off the field. Amongst the roar of the crowd, Traci waved bravely.

Job walked over and placed his hand on Disney's shoulder. "Hey, maybe it won't be so bad."

An instant replay of the hit flashed on the screen. Madden circled the injury on the screen as he explained, *Oh, this isn't going to be good. See that part where the ankle and calf meet, that's a cankle injury, and a cankle injury of this magnitude could end your season.*

Michaels answered. *Isn't that area called the tibia?*

Madden denied—*No, no, it's definitely a cankle.*

Disney wiped the tears from her cheeks. Her posture became rigid as she glanced across the room. Her eyes looked at the PlayStation with disdain. "If you didn't make that play, *who* did?"

Job's jaw was clenched with stubborn determination as his eyes followed Disney's. Slowly, he relaxed and took a deep breath. "I hate saying this, and I know you don't want to hear it, but the person who made that play was your dad."

...

Later that evening, Branson pulled into his driveway with a deep frown and furrowed brow. His expression lifted at the sight of his daughter waiting for him on the porch. Years ago, Branson had contemplated and did eventually satiate a "Tip" type using the same "Tip" leverage. He had done it to obtain what they all sought: "Tip" power. His grandfather, finding out about it, had cautioned him, "You can't make a deal with the devil without breaking the most important deal you've made with yourself, like what you will and won't do for money." Maybe, his grandfather might have been willing to make an exception if he had known it was the only way to protect his family.

Branson stepped out of the SUV and walked to the porch. He bent over to hug Disney, but she stood cold and stiff.

Branson stepped back with a questioning expression.

"What are you doing out here?" he asked.

"Why did you miss that block?"

Branson looked at his daughter, nodded slightly, and started with, "It was such an unexpected play, that DE came out of nowhe…"

"Dad. Don't."

Branson knew she knew. He paused, took a deep breath and then sat down on the porch steps. "Disney, I want to tell you the truth, but I can't."

With her hands braced on her hips, she looked less like his little girl and more like a superhero prepared for battle.

"I don't believe you," Disney answered.

"One day I will tell you the truth, but for now, I just need you to trust me."

"You need me to trust you? You! The person that literally just ended Traci's first season. Maybe her career! How could you? That was me on the field! You tried to destroy me!"

Unbeknownst to Branson, Disney wasn't speaking metaphorically.

"And now you sit here looking like you're a victim. What else don't I know? In what other ways are you against me? I always assumed because you were with my mom, you had to be down but hell, she is dope so it's not like you sacrificed anything by marrying her. You actually came up! It's like somebody patting themselves on the back for voting for Obama. He was the most qualified candidate. Why wouldn't you? What else are you not telling me? What's in your heart?"

Disney glared at her father. He looked forward and avoided eye contact. Branson would have preferred a staring contest with Medusa or goggle the Ark of the Covenant.

"I believed you were different. But you are just like all the rest of them… all those other people who don't believe someone can play football if they have a pu—."

"Disney!" Branson interrupted.

"Vagina," Disney sneered.

"I'm still your dad."

"You're my father. Can't change that. But I don't have a dad."

"Now Disney..." Branson started to dispute her proclamation but she had already stormed back inside the house. "Sometimes in life you have to behave like a coward to be a hero for your family."

"Everybody's got to do what they've got to do."
~Tom Osborne, Head Coach Nebraska Cornhuskers

It took three days after Sunday's game for Cleo and Billie to meet up at the practice facility's theater. Monday had been out as Billie, like most coaches, gave players the next day off after a win. Tuesday had also been a no go as it was a mandatory off-day per the Collective Bargaining Agreement. So Wednesday it was, and Cleo was not complaining. She needed time to process.

Surrounded by darkness, they watched replay after replay of the missed block. Each time, Cleo hoped to catch some tiny detail that she had missed previously: a slip, a fumble, anything to change her mind about what she had seen. No such explanation came. "This just doesn't make sense. Why would he do that?"

Billie's stern frown deepened. She had a few thoughts on the subject but none that she was willing yet to consciously acknowledge much less vocalize or share. "I don't know, and now no one is talking."

"You don't think..." Cleo paused. Tip was a despicable waste of a human being, but surely he wouldn't risk injuring one of his own. Then again, you don't earn 'waste of a human being' status without doing some really repugnant shit.

Billie hit the pause button. "The team physician has said that Traci will be out of commission for at least 4 weeks. They are beginning rehab this afternoon. We'll have to play it by ear."

Or a magical video game console or it was never a break in the first place.

Cleo reached across the table for the caramel latte she had picked up on her way to work this morning. By now it was cold and not nearly as satisfying as usual. "What does this mean for next week?"

"We have no other choice than to put in Tracy."

A sour expression crossed Cleo's face. "Reward the man who might be responsible for this?"

"We don't know anything for certain at this point." Nor, Billie suspected, would they know in the immediate future. Tensions had been riding high at this morning's practice from both the players and the staff. It was insubordination, plain and simple. And at the practice, she had treated the players accordingly. If she could not make them talk, she would make them pay... and pay they did. Maybe a few more practices that left them crawling off the field would loosen their lips?

...

A part of Branson enjoyed the brutal practice routine. Pushing his body to the limits and beyond ebbed the guilt that seemed to magnify with each passing day. For as long as Branson could remember, he had always felt ashamed of having feelings. Growing up, there had been no question in his mind that what he felt was wrong, unnatural. If he had ever doubted it, his father would remind him with a strong backhand. Though his father never knew for certain, Branson knew he had his suspicions. For years, he had tried to fight it and be the man his father wanted him to be. Denying himself his identity had worked well. Until he moved away for college. That's when he fell in love for the first time, but it was short-lived: there was too much pressure both on the field and off for the relationship to last.

A few years later, Debbie came into his life. Shortly after, Disney was born. Life as a family man changed him. All that he thought he wanted slipped away like a recollection of a distant dream. Occasionally, memories of that forgotten time would creep inside his mind. They made him feel warm, like remembering a perfect summer day when all felt right. But inevitably, guilt and fear always crashed with the vengeance of a pop-up storm. If he was a few years younger and 10% cooler, his subconscious would start playing Donald Glover's *It Feels Like Summer* whenever he thought of this tragically wonderful time. To make up for all that he lacked as a husband, Branson tried to be the best father he knew how to be. He never wanted Disney to feel his shame. It worked. In her eyes, he was everything that his father made him believe a man should be. Until last Sunday. He could see it on her face every time she looked at him. He could hear his father speaking through his only child. *You're a coward. You'll never be a real man.* Now, he did not know what was worse, Disney learning the truth, or that he had made her believe a lie for so long.

...

Surrounded by a team physio, Cleo, Billie, and Shawn, Traci was standing on her injured foot with her arms stretched out to her sides.

"Twenty-five, twenty-six, twenty-seven..."

When Traci started to wobble, Billie stepped forward. "You're doing great."

Crouching over, Shawn's hands rested on his thighs. "Twenty-nine, thirty... half-way there... What are you doing here?"

Poised like a high wire performer, Traci's upper body whirled around to see who he was talking to. The sudden movement did not mix well with her unsteady foot. Trying to regain her balance, her arms whirled about like a helicopter seed parachuting from a maple tree. She closed her eyes and braced for a painful meet and greet with the ground arranged by the undefeated matchmaker... gravity. When no painful impact occurred, she opened her eyes to find herself rescued and cradled in Shawn's outstretched arms. Shawn & Traci 1, gravity 0.

Billie stepped between them and Branson, who no one had noticed hovering in the doorway. His massive frame filled the space. She motioned for him to come over more as a courtesy to the other people who were trying to come in and out. "Landover, fancy seeing you here."

"I just wanted to see how it was going."

Flustered and embarrassed, Traci tried to stand on her own, but she noticed that Shawn held his hand on her waist in what seemed like an almost protective gesture. "Branson."

Branson stepped forward. "I wasn't expecting a cheering section. I didn't mean to interrupt or anything."

The physical therapist slid a chair over and helped Traci sit down. "We were just getting ready to take a short break."

Traci glanced around her entourage with a guarded expression. "I don't need a break."

"I appreciate your commitment, but you can't over do it."

Feeling like a third wheel, a very much unwanted third wheel, Branson looked at the others cautiously. Then he looked at Traci. "Since you've got a moment, I was wondering if we could talk... alone."

Billie motioned for Cleo to follow her to the other side of the room. Not as easily convinced, Shawn held his ground until Traci reached for his hand. "Give us a sec, okay."

Branson walked over and pulled up another bench and then sat down in front of her. "Look, I just wanted to apologize. What happened... what I did was not right. I know that now, and I promise it won't ever happen again. As long as we are on the same team, it's ride or die."

It hurt. Traci could not pretend otherwise. "I thought we were ride or die. Why should I believe you now?"

Branson leaned forward with his hands resting under his chin. His eyes were focused on her face, but Traci knew he wasn't really looking at her, but through her to some distant and troubling point in the future. "Things happened. I got backed into a corner and made the wrong decision."

"Who? Who is threatening you?"

"If I tell you, then you're going to make the wrong decision. Just know that I'm not going to let that happen again. I'm dealing with it. You don't have to believe me now, but I'm going to prove it to you. I need to talk to Billie and Cleo."

Traci gently grabbed Branson's hands. She looked at the palms, the fingers, the nail beds, cradled each individually like they were infant twins and together like they were one in the same, equally innocent or guilty. Traci stared Branson in the eye.

"They say forgiveness is for the victim and not the perpetrator. Heard Oprah speak about it once. Said she was walking down the Miracle Mile in Chicago and saw someone she had been mad at for years. Oprah said she got mad all over again. It had been years since she had seen this person yet she was still mad like it was only yesterday. But the person she was angry at was walking around, smiling and happy. Oprah thought, "Here I am upset and this person is walking around happy not thinking about me. While I'm walking around mad as hell!""

Branson laughed.

"So I understand your thought process. Even why you may have done what you did. Although because you are all like a secret squirrel, something doesn't add up. You remind me of a character in a movie—an action movie. The one where someone does whatever is necessary—no matter how immoral—to protect their child. They betray their friends, and fortunately the heroes still save the day and forgives their friend that deceived them or didn't tell them he was being blackmailed. All because, well, he or she was trying to protect their child."

Branson nodded in agreement. Traci wiped a building tear from her eye with her shoulder. She dropped Branson's hands.

"I'm not Oprah and this ain't a movie. I'm fine with my

anger. She wasn't angry 24/7—only when she saw the person that she didn't like. Anger is my body's way of producing psychological antibodies. I don't believe everyone should be forgiven. Nor do I believe that you do whatever is necessary to protect loved ones even if it means you become as evil as the ones you seek to protect them from. My life is not a plot twist, uh what do they call it a story device for you or your family's so called protection."

"So walk on your two perfectly good legs and talk to Cleo and Billie. I will start limping in that direction. By the time I get there you should be done. Then I will have my meeting with Cleo and Billie to let them know that we talked. That I forgive you and…"

Branson exhaled.

"And they should put your ass on the trading block or find themselves another running back. I will retire before I play another game on the same team as you. Now get the hell out of my face."

"Traci—" Branson cried.

"GO!"

Branson slowly rose and walked toward the exit. As he headed down the hall, he could hear the sounds of Traci's crutches scraping the floor as she made her way behind him.

...

Of the two, Cleo was less shaken by Branson's revelation. "Branson, is your family supportive of this decision?"

Billie surmised that Cleo could afford to be more sympathetic because she was not the one who had to work out the logistics of the situation. "We need to take a second before we jump the gun."

Branson looked back and forth between his team's owner and his coach. The first time he had come out, he was young and in love with a boy. It wasn't any easier then, but this time felt different. It felt freeing. Since he made his decision, he had been dreading the moment when they would look at him like he was suddenly a different person, but that moment never came. "Coach... I'm tired. I'm tired of feeling shameful. I'm tired of people using who I am against me. My wife has known for years, and I figure, if God can make room for people like me in her world..."

Billie's troubled expression lifted to a smile.

"...Then the NFL can make room for people like me in their ..."

"Not theirs... ours... yours. The world of football belongs to you as much as it does them," Billie interjected.

Billie and Branson looked deep into each other's eyes... nodded in agreement and shook hands.

Cleo threw up her hands. "No hugs?" She tried to put her arms around Billie and Branson, but they both walked away before she could complete her hug. She was left standing there, unhugged.

"That's so wrong. So wrong!" Cleo decided to hug herself. A dreamy smile filled her face. "Ahhhh never waste a good hug."

Branson and Billie smiled and shook their heads in judgement at Cleo's very public display of literal self-love reminiscent of the hippie she had once been just a few short months ago.

"If my mother put on a helmet and shoulder pads and a uniform that wasn't the same as the one I was wearing, I'd run over her if she was in my way. And I love my mother."
~Bo Jackson, Running Back, Los Angeles Raiders

Disney sat alone in the back corner of the school cafeteria. Knowing that it was her favorite meal, the kitchen staff had heaped an oversized portion of chicken and noodles on her lunch tray. But today, she couldn't eat a bite. Instead, she mixed it all together until her tray resembled chicken, green bean, mash potato, fruit cup vomit.

Job strolled over and sat down. He grimaced at the sight of her food art. "If you weren't hungry, I would have eaten it for you."

"Leave me alone." Disney pushed the tray away and cradled her head in her hands.

Ignoring her, Job sat down. He knew what was bothering her. Most likely a large majority of the students in school did too. Branson's public announcement had been just as unexpected as it was shocking. "Disney… look, I'm sorry. I didn't know."

"You think I did? It's that stupid game. It has ruined everything."

"Not everything." Job leaned over the table. "I've been

giving it a lot of thought, and I know the game is powerful, but it did not make your dad…"

Even though she wanted nothing more than to be invisible at the moment, she pushed her hoodie away from her face. "Say it, Job. Just say it!"

"It didn't make your dad gay. Wait, let me rephrase that. It didn't make your dad injure Traci and decide to come out. I mean live his truth. Yeah, live his truth."

Two boys walked past their table. One nudged the other, and they both stopped. "Hey Disney, did you get to meet your dad's new *boyfriend* yet?"

Job sat up. With a clenched fist, he answered angrily, "Leave her alone."

The boys started laughing. Their exchange captured the attention of several onlookers. A circle of curiosity began to form around the table.

"You know what I think, Job," one of the boys called out, "I think you're queer too. That's why you spend all your time hanging out with a girl."

Disney sat up and looked at Job. She had seen him angry and frustrated before but never like this. Her heart began to race, and she reached for his hand. "It's not worth it."

"That don't even make sense. Wouldn't I hang out with another dude? Why am I even trying to apply logic to your stupid ass comments? Like I… said… leave her alone," Job gritted through his teeth.

"You want some of this, pause."

Job knew where this was going. The word pause was said after something that may be taken as homosexual to make it clear that the person speaking is not gay. It wasn't cool and today of all days, it could push someone like Job over the edge. Job took a deep breath and stared into Disney's eyes. She smiled and the world for a moment was alright, hakuna matata.

"Huh? You didn't hear me? What you gonna do about it, gay boy?" the boy challenged.

"Ohhhh, I see. You want smoke. Well, you got the right one today," Job accepted.

In a flash, Job leaped over the table and the boy was on the ground. Job slapped the boy with the back of his hand. The next thing Job knew he was being held down, face smashed against the floor, by a school security guard. He glanced up and saw the instigator surrounded by a couple teachers and the school principal. He couldn't remember the details but knew he had gotten at least a serious pimp slap in because the boy's nose was bleeding. The brief spark of pride he felt was snuffed out by the sight of Disney's tears.

"He didn't start it," Disney sobbed.

As Job was being hauled up off the ground, the principal pointed his finger towards Disney. "You need to come down to the office too. We need to sort this mess and decide if assault charges need to be filed."

"It was completely unprovoked, sir," the boy's friend claimed as they were marched single-file out of the cafeteria with Job and the security guard holding up the rear, "we were just walking by on the way to our table and he just went insane…"

At just that moment, someone in the crowd yelled.

"I got the whole thing on my phone from the moment they started teasing Disney!"

...

Billie blew the whistle and then bellowed, "Lamb, over here!"

Shawn took off his helmet and jogged over expecting some sort of critical analysis of his play. Billie was not a coach for the thin-skinned, that was for certain. Her hawk eyes saw everything and she wasn't the type who prettied up her words and left the harsh stuff for the offensive coordinator. She called it like she saw it and didn't care who was around to hear. She was not like some of his previous coaches, who danced around egos. Her blunt-edged words bothered some players, but Shawn respected her more for it.

"What is it, Coach?"

"Front office just called down. There has been some sort of altercation at your son's school, and they said you needed to come right away."

Confused, Shawn shook his head. "Altercation? What happened?"

"They didn't say, but you had better go down there and figure it out," Billie advised.

Altercation. It just did not make sense. Shawn would just as soon expect to hear that Santa Claus was stuck on top of his roof as to hear that his son had been in some sort of fight. By the time he had changed his clothes and was driving to school, his confusion gave way to fear. What if Job had been hurt? His fear was on the verge of becoming full-fledged panic when he realized that if Job had been seriously injured, he would have been told to go to the hospital instead of the school, but still…

Several minutes later, Shawn was sitting in an office with his son on one side of the desk and the principal on the other. Shawn had not been in a principal's office since he was in high school, but back then he had been a real hot head and spent so much time there that it almost felt a little like going home.

Principal Warner presented the facts, after which Job remained quiet and sullen, neither affirming nor denying the accusations. It reminded Shawn of him at that age. Job was lucky though that it was not his grandfather that was sitting beside him. He would have whacked him over the head just for being called to the school in the first place.

"Well… Job, what have you got to say for yourself?" Shawn asked, trying to sound like a mature adult. When Job remained silent, he continued, "So it's like that? You think just because some kid called you gay that you have the right to punch him in the face?"

"It was a slap, not a punch."

"What the hell is the difference?"

Job half-heartedly demonstrated a punch then a

backhand. Shawn fought back a laugh that almost escaped his lips.

"So what? Even if you were, so what! Do you know how many names I've been called? If I punched or slapped everyone that has ever disrespected me, I'd be in prison now. You know better than that, son."

Principal Warner cleared his throat, leaned forward, and rested his folded hands on the desk. Shawn recognized the familiar position and wondered if they taught that in college. With his sternest stance, Warner said, "We have a zero tolerance for bullying and fighting in this school. As such, Job will be given a five-day suspension, and if this type of behavior happens again, he will face expulsion."

Shawn looked on thoughtfully and slowly nodded his head. "I respect that. Can I ask what about the other student involved? Will he also be given a five-day suspension as well?"

"Because of confidentiality, I'm not at liberty to discuss the other student's possible consequences."

"Well, until you can prove that the other student will be punished more severely for the hate speech he used to oppress my son, Job will not be suspended. And if that is a problem, we can discuss the matter on ESPN next time I give an interview."

Shawn pulled out his phone.

"Ah, look at that, I'm scheduled to appear tomorrow. Are we good?" Shawn said, as if it were a statement.

"Given the totality of the circumstances, I don't see any need for Job to be suspended."

Job flashed a quick grin.

Shawn's eyes narrowed with suspicion at both of them. Plenty of things to say came to mind, but instead, he decided to make this a teachable moment for his son. "Job will voluntarily spend the next 14 lunch periods in this office with you studying. You both could benefit from a little forced discomfort."

Job and the principal frowned.

...

Since the press conference, several broadcasters had forecasted that the Lions' record-breaking season was about to come to an abrupt halt. Several factors were at play. First, Traci, darling of the NFL, was out with injury. Second, they predicted that Branson Landover, the first openly known gay man to play in a regular season game, was bound to cause protests and boycotts i.e. be a distraction. This was a given considering they were playing in the heart of the Bible Belt in Nissan Stadium, home of the Tennessee Titans. People were more understanding these days, but people were also less understanding these days.

Now that he was publicly out, a few of the players had become standoffish, but most of them were supportive. Branson believed Shawn had a lot to do with that. As quarterback and leader of the team, the players naturally looked at him and gauged their responses based off his. Come to find out, Shawn had a gay uncle who had gay friends, and he had spent a lot of time around them growing up, so Branson's announcement was not a big deal to him.

Knowing he had the support of his team and his wife, or soon-to-be former wife/lifelong friend, meant a lot to him. Maybe one day he would have the support of his only child as well, but right now he could only face one battle at a time. Branson had no intention of facing it alone. Sitting by himself in the locker room, he offered up a quick prayer because despite what protesters believed, he knew that God had made him this way for a purpose, and hiding behind shame and guilt was not it.

Shawn walked over and nudged Branson on the shoulder. "You ready, Big Guy?"

"About ready as I'll ever be."

They walked together out of the locker room. On the way to the field, Shawn started to give a pep talk. "No matter what is out there, you can't let it get to your head. Some people are always going to hate... sometimes for no reason at all...

you've got to..."

Shawn's words fell short. Branson's eyes grew wondrous at the sight that greeted him. He had expected to see more than a few posters and signs with hateful rhetoric, but instead he discovered a large-scale, coordinated gay rights demonstration. Fans wearing red, orange, yellow, green, blue, indigo, and violet Lions' T-shirts filled the stadium.

Shawn laughed and slapped Branson's shoulder. "It's cool that the rainbow is the symbol. It's like a message that all are welcome. The rainbow army has shut out the protestors. We better give them something good to cheer for."

"It's pretty simple for me; I believe all people are created equal, regardless of their sexuality. To promote respect and acceptance is an important role for NFL players and the NFLPA."
~Steve Gleason, Safety, New Orleans Saints

Disney sat like a crumpled piece of fuchsia-colored construction paper that was about to be swallowed whole by Job's massive white sofa. She looked just as miserable. Job wished more than anything that he could find a way to iron out all her creases and make everything go back to the way it was, but he knew that sometimes it was impossible. People are just like paper. They could bend and sway in the wind but once folded, the crease never goes away.

He walked across the room and sat a bowl down in front of her. "Brownie *á la* mode."

Disney picked up the dish. Her spoon toyed with the vanilla ice cream, but she could not bring herself to lift it up to her lips. Ever since the family meeting, her stomach had been in knots. Of all possibilities in the entire universe, she was hit by one that she never saw coming.

Job sat down beside her. His distance was a little further than usual. "You need to eat something."

Disney noticed that he seemed extra cautious since

she had arrived. She wondered if he thought she was now breakable or contagious. "I'm not hungry." Disney sat the bowl down on the table.

"You know… there are worse things."

Hot tears started leaking from her eyes. She swiped at them with a vengeance. Her mom had said the same thing and promised that they would always be a family no matter what. *Yeah, a family with one mom and three dads: her biological father, and two step-dads.* Disney reasoned that she could have handled the situation better if they were just getting divorced. A lot of her friends' parents had gotten divorced. A few even claimed that they preferred it because now they did not have to listen to all the fights, plus they got double Christmases. But Disney did not want two Christmases, and her parents never fought. They were best friends. They *had* the perfect family. They had lived a lie this long. Why did that have to change now that they were living the truth?

"Sorry, I can't think of any at the moment," snapped Disney.

"For starters," Job said, "one of your parents could have died."

"At this point, that would almost be preferable. At least I would not have to be *Disney with the gay dad, the beard mom, on everybody's feed with comments.*"

Job started shaking his head in vehement denial. "You don't mean that. I'd give anything to see my mom again. I wouldn't care if she were a lesbian or wanted to become a man for that matter. I would love the hell out of a trans dad."

Job's passionate response slipped past Disney's veil of misery. Maybe he was right? No, she knew he was right. No matter what, Disney loved her father and did not even want to think about the day when he would no longer be on this earth.

Disney picked up the dessert dish. Tiny bites were all she could stomach. Given his response at school, she was reluctant to tell Job the whole truth. But if she could not talk to Job, who could she talk to? "This week hasn't been easy."

Job tensed up. "Have any other students approached you?"

Disney cast him a sideways glance. "A few… not a lot. In gym class, a group of boys pointed at me and started laughing, but then later a kid I never met from seventh grade came up to me and said he thought my dad was really brave."

"He's probably gay."

Disney's expression turned to outrage at his off-hand remark.

"No, not like he can't think your dad is brave unless he is a gay. Not *a* gay. I mean gay. You're not alone."

Job bit his lip as he regrouped.

"Think about it, Disney… just think. You can't be the only student in school that has a homosexual parent, and we both know there are gay students who are too afraid to come out. Even these days. I mean we may see all this pro-gay stuff on IG, hear people talk about acceptance, express support for trans people, but what we aren't seeing is the everyday hate that doesn't fit into the "we've gotten past the homophobic narrative" that the media wants to tell. Maybe if more people like your dad were honest about who they are and who they love, it wouldn't be a big deal anymore?"

Disney nodded her head in agreement then let out a five stage sigh that grew from a disturbance to a depression to a storm to a hurricane and finally dissipated into honesty.

"Imma keep it a 100 with you Job."

"Go ahead, keep it a buck!"

They both laughed.

"It's just so damn messy. Debbie and Branson. Yes, I'm on a first name basis with both of them now!"

Job and Disney chuckled. Disney continued, "Debbie and Branson make it seem like the only reason they aren't together is because he is gay."

Disney stared into space for a few moments.

"I don't care if he is gay. I'm in my feelings about how this affects me. I want them to stay together. That's it. I want to live in the house with my dad!" Disney said, as tears skydived from her eyes.

"I want to post pictures and be able to turn my comments on without people talking shit. I just want to scroll my feed without seeing tweets about my family. I just want to be a kid. It's difficult to give support when you feel like you have none. Right now it feels like it is my family against the world."

Job raised Disney's crying face by her chin until their eyes locked. Inches from her lips Job traversed slowly. He turned to bridge the gap between him and her tears, kissed each one of them, and ended the trip with what Disney needed the most—a long, tender hug.

Job gave Disney one last squeeze and then flipped on the television to catch some of the pre-game coverage. He already knew who was going to win and had a pretty good idea how many points they would win by. But he thought the other side of the story might also be interesting. Plus given that they now had to fend off two extinction level trade events, they couldn't take any chances. First, they needed to win in such a way that no one would want to trade their dads. Second, they needed to win so convincingly that Traci would want to stay and compete for a Super Bowl berth.

As the cameras panned across the stadium, Michaels' voice could be heard saying, *"Well folks, I'm not sure how many times I've said it this season, but this is a first."*

Madden answered, *"You know, I'm not sure now. Going into this season, detractors claimed the Lions were out to break the rules, but maybe they just wanted to redefine them. To date, there have been eleven known gay players in NFL history. Michael Sam made national news in 2014 when he announced that he was gay before the NFL draft. He was drafted by the St. Louis Rams but was released after playing all four preseason games. No known... out gay NFL player has ever played in a regular season game. Going into this game, there were speculations of protests and boycotts, but that's not what I'm seeing folks."*

Disney's hands covered her mouth. Her eyes grew wide with wonder at the sight of the gigantic rainbow wall of fans.

Job chuckled. "Looks like your family is bigger than you thought."

...

Cleo looked at Tip. He was sweating profusely and looked to be in the midst of having a major coronary. She nodded towards the red AED machine hanging on the wall. "I'm ready if you need it," she snarked.

Tip wiped his brow with a tissue. "I hope this makes you happy."

"Of course, it does." Cleo laughed. "Only a heartless troll doesn't like a rainbow. Think about this, Tip, there is always a pot of gold under a rainbow, and there is no doubt in my mind that *you* will manage to get your hands on it."

Tip's hand stilled. He pushed the tissue inside his pocket and reached for his phone. Some people required stents and bypass surgeries to recover. Tip just needed to hear the promise of more money. "Tip here. Say, for next week's game how about you send over a couple queer homeless bums... what do you mean you don't know if they are queer... I'll tell you what, say I throw in a couple extra hundred dollars but they have to be in full regalia, I don't want any half-ass homos..."

Cleo sank low in her chair and covered her face with her hands in shame and a huge helping of mortification. *Got to get rid of this guy.*

Branson's eyes swept across the defense like a QR reader scanning a code for free money. He was locked in and focused. Shawn moved his left leg and Tracy went in motion shifting closer to Branson's side.

Branson took in a deep breath. Before he could expel it, the ball was snapped and Tracy was running his way... fast. Real fast. Tracy was expecting a hole. A big hole. Branson knew it too as he could hear Tracy's footsteps behind him come closer... fast.

Two linebackers were in his way. Branson knew he could take one, but block both? Naw. At least not without skirting the line. Branson grabbed the first linebacker and turned him right. The LB tried to break away but Branson's hands held two handfuls full of jersey...outside of the refs' lines of sight.

Like a judo master dancing the Black Swan ballet, Branson guided the LB into a gracefully violent collision with the second LB. They all collided with the ground like they were taking dirty naps.

Whoa, look at that hole! You could fit a small planet through that thing. Like Pluto! John said.

Pluto isn't a planet anymore, John.

Well, if it were a planet, it would fit through there.

Tracy went from prey to predator in an instant as he hopped through the celestial-sized hole like an interstellar jackrabbit and then transformed into the off-spring of a comet and cheetah, sprinting to the end zone.

John, was that holding? Al Michaels said more as a statement.

Well, technically the ref could call holding on every play. Landover can get away with that twice or three times a game. Especially in the first quarter before the refs have the chance to look at the tape and see how they did the first quarter.

Tracy reached out his hand to give Branson a handshake that would likely lead to a man hug fit for long lost brothers reunited. But Branson left him hanging and headed to the sideline. Tracy tried to play it off by spinning into a celebratory dance move. When he finished, he saw Billie staring at him with narrowed eyes. Billie nodded knowingly and stared him down all the way into the tunnel.

At halftime, the team and coaching staff were clustered together in the locker room. Billie believed this precious time should be used to address points of weakness and concerns. Save the accolades for after we win... the Super Bowl.

The defensive coordinator had just finished. The offensive coordinator was up next. Billie, standing just behind the players ready to interject anything she thought might be important, noticed a large shadow figure lingering in the hall. She motioned for him to step forward. "Stan, do you have anything to add?"

The players looked surprised but knew better than to say anything.

"The TE's hands looked a little loose when he was handling the ball," Stan offered.

Billie nodded. "I thought the same thing myself. Remember boys, just because we are undefeated doesn't mean that we can't lose. Don't get it in your heads that you are unstoppable because you aren't! We can't get sloppy now."

As the team exited the locker room, Billie and Stan stayed behind. Knowing she didn't have much time, Stan quickly handed Billie a manila envelope. Billie hurriedly placed the envelope in her bag.

"You going to even look at them?"

Billie reached out and hugged Stan.

They hugged each other like two people with a universe of history and no future.

...

During the fourth quarter, the commentators debated the final plays of the game. Michaels started. *The Lions have a two point lead with 58 seconds left on the clock.*

Madden added, *And a two point lead in a situation like this isn't any better than a one point lead because if the other team makes a field goal before that clock hits zero, you still go home with an L.*

With no ability to bounce back.

What's that Al? John asked, confused.

Al replied—*Nothing, nothing John.*

The Titan's QB called an audible. The RB and FB went in opposite motion, but the Twins didn't move. When the ball was hiked both Twins came around the corner fast and tight like two motorcycles. They sandwiched the QB like giant clapping hands at a Beyoncé concert.

Wow! If I didn't know better, I would have thought those two guys were in the huddle, Madden said.

The ball popped out and the Twins fell on it. Literally they both fell on it simultaneously. They fought for the ball briefly and Uno took it as the intensity of the fight subsided when they realized they were on the same team.

Now that's a smart play. They both fell on the ball. These guys are in sync. When they are done in the NFL, they may want to explore synchronized swimming. If you're up two with the ball and 20 seconds left, you might as well be up 200 because when the clock runs down... Madden's voice trails off.

...

A win was a win was a win, but this one did not feel as victorious without Traci by Shawn's side. He knew better than to let the media on to his discontentment. After Cleo's now infamous press conference, the media had given them all a little space, but there were still a few land sharks hiding amongst the journalists. Sniffing around for fresh blood. Sniffing for stories beyond football.

Shawn would be the first to admit that in the past, he had not done himself any favors. If some of the media that covered him were carnivores, he had tossed them more than his fair share of bloody meat. Despite slip-ups here and there, he was trying to be a better man. He did not really understand it, but lately, he had had a feeling that he had been given a second chance. And not just on the field. Second chances don't come along every day, and Shawn was not about to squander it.

Instead of saying how he really felt, Shawn stood smiling beside Tracy as he was once again playing star. A part of Shawn felt sorry for Tracy. He had been like Tracy once—had a good woman and drove her away. Right now in his glory, Tracy still probably didn't realize what he had lost, but he would one day. By then it would be too late.

Branson walked past. The reporter called out his

name. Most of the time, he pretended not to hear, but today he stopped. At the end of the day, many reporters were just doing their jobs. Not to mention they were evangelists of the game. *Without them promoting the game, these TV contracts that paid him might be way more delicate.* Shawn waved him forward. "Get over there, Big Guy."

Branson's feet moved like he was trudging through a swamp filled with molasses.

The reporter held the mic in front of him. "Branson, do you have anything to say?"

"I… just want to say thanks for all the support. It means a lot."

The reporter knew he was not going to get any more from Branson, so she decided to go to Shawn, who always had something to say.

"Shawn, do you feel Branson's announcement has caused any contention for the team?"

Shawn leaned over the microphone with a thoughtful expression. "Announcement… what announcement?"

The reporter chuckled nervously. "Last week, Branson announced that he would be the first homosexual NFL player to play in a regular season game."

Shawn dropped his hand from Branson's shoulder as if he had been struck by lightning. Looking flabbergasted, he yelled, "You're what?" A wide smile cracked Shawn's face as he reached once again for Branson's shoulder and pulled him close. "Nah, I'm just playing. It ain't like that. We're a team, and more importantly, Branson is my friend. Just between you and me… and the rest of the world, I think what he did took more courage and bravery than most of the rest of us muster our entire lives. I've got nothing but respect."

"When you win, nothing hurts."
~Joe Namath, Quarterback, New York Jets

After three more Lion victories, Traci was given a clean bill of health by the team physicians. Any lingering hope she had of salvaging her relationship was demolished as soon as Tracy realized he would be once again be warming the bench. His childish antics evaporated the last of her sorrow, and soon she began to wonder what she had ever seen in him in the first place.

If that wasn't enough, she had to decide how to follow through on her threat, rather, her promise to demand a trade, and refuse to take the field if Branson was still on the roster. To make a tense situation more taut, her heart had started to become inextricably linked with the man that many thought was the Lions' heart, Shawn Lamb.

Traci always heard that when one door closes another one opens. Some miracles are more complicated than others. Shawn was her friend, though lately he had started to feel like something more. Fresh from a broken engagement, she did not give it much of a thought when they started spending more time together off the field than on. It wasn't until she was sitting in Shawn's kitchen with him and his son and noticed how natural it felt that she decided to hit the brakes.

Once burnt… she half-expected Shawn to start behaving like Tracy, but he did not. Shawn respected her distance, which made her realize he deserved an explanation. One afternoon after practice, she caught up with him on the field. "Look, just so you know, I'm not trying to ghost you. I don't play games like that."

Shawn's playful half-grin didn't falter. "I was wondering if it was something I said."

Traci could not quite meet his eyes. She tucked her head and shook it in denial. "It's not like that… or anything against you or your son. I'm not looking for a rebound… or an instant replay. Right now, I just need to focus on my game."

Shawn gave her a thoughtful expression. "I get that."

"You do?"

"Sure, you need a break between seasons. It's a tough game to play."

Traci laughed. "Love or football?"

Shawn pondered for a moment.

"Yes."

They both chuckled. The laughter trailed off and all that was left was the longing stare they shared.

"Well, it's getting late," Traci said as she made her way slowly to the door. Shawn sauntered behind her. As she crossed the threshold with her back to him, Shawn reached for a kiss, but alas she was too far. When she turned around, his courage—like the laughter—dissipated as unused courage tends to do. He replaced it with real talk.

"Serious, I suppose both, but here's the thing, they are both a whole lot easier when you have the right person by your side. Rest up, and when you're ready, give me a call."

Traci smiled and raised her phone. As she went in to give him a kiss, it rang. Traci looked at the screen and her brow wrinkled.

"What area code is 615?"

"Tennessee. That's Billie."

Traci tried to swipe up to answer but the call dropped and a text came through. Traci teared up.

"What does it say?"

Traci smiled and flashed Shawn the screen.

Found a time machine. Got some equity for you.

...

"Let me guess, another win," Disney said, as she settled into Job's sofa while balancing a large bowl of popcorn on her lap.

Job handed her some napkins as she had insisted on dousing the popcorn with melted butter. He did not mind a little butter himself, but too much was overkill. It was kind of ironic that Disney thought the same thing, only she did not have the popcorn in mind. "That's a joke, right?" quipped Job.

They both knew they were past the point where defeat was an option. It was the first week of playoffs.

Disney munched on her popcorn. In between bites, she answered, "Maybe."

Job looked at her like she had lost her mind. He turned on the PlayStation. A system update message scrolled across the screen. "You've got to be kidding me." Job hit the X button. While he waited, he flashed Disney a look. "I know you're kidding. If we lose now, what was the point of the whole season?"

"Hmm... I don't know, Job, maybe so your dad wouldn't get traded. Or did you forget that already?"

Job hit the X button again. "Come on." He was growing increasingly frustrated with both the game and Disney. "It must be frozen," he grumbled under his breath. Job walked over and turned off the game system, waited fifteen seconds, and turned it on again.

Once again, a system update message flashed across the screen. "Come on! Don't do this now."

Disney's casual disinterest gave way to something more elemental. She leaned forward. "What's happening?"

Job paced across the living room like a caged tiger. "I don't know… nothing."

Several minutes passed. In a panic, Job tried once again to restart the system, but nothing changed. On the other television screen, players were taking the field. The Indianapolis Colts won the coin toss and opted to receive.

"Is there a number on the back we can call?" Disney asked.

"GameStop doesn't have technicians who work on magic PlayStations."

"Smart ass, maybe it's not a magic issue but a hardware issue."

"My bad."

"So what are we going to do?"

Job sat down on the sofa. Leaning back, he placed his hands over his face. "I don't know… maybe pray."

...

Al Michaels announced—*John is it me or has this been an incredible game. An offensive game to say the least.*

John answered—*Yes it has! After almost four quarters, I can't believe the score is zero to zero!*

John, the score is 42 to 42. If either team scores three more points, this game will tie the fourth place record of highest points scored in a playoff that was set by the Jaguars and Steelers in January 2018. Folks, we just don't see these kinds of numbers every day.

If the score is tied, Al, it might as well be zero to zero.

Traci grabbed her helmet and gingerly started toward the end zone to receive the kickoff. Billie noticed her slow movements and grabbed her by the arm.

Looks like Coach Wall is giving her starter some last minute advice.—Al said.

Who can blame her? With twenty-seconds left on the clock, this could end up being the Lions franchise ending defeat. Given the rumors anything short of a Super Bowl win could mean a sell. You just *never know. You think you will get back here but the game is so hard on the body. —*John spewed ominously.

Are you at all surprised at Traci's durability, John?

This young lady has really been smart avoiding hits, sliding, and just overall minimizing contact. And with that All Pro O line, she doesn't take big hits, which is rare for a running back.

Billie looked Traci in the eyes. "Are you injured or are you hurt?"

"I'm. I'm okay Coach."

"Not the way you're walking around here. I've seen high turtles move faster. So are you injured or hurt?"

"I don't know."

Billie used her iPad to shield her lips from the cameras. "Are you in pain?"

"No. I mean... I mean yes! I mean remind me what's the difference between hurt and injured?"

"If you're hurt, you can still play? If you're injured, you can't. So are you hurt or injured?"

Traci doubled over and fell to one knee. Billie crouched beside her and bowed her head. "*What is it?* Your ribs? Did you puncture a lung?

"No, I'm cramping. It's that time."

Bewildered, Billie had seen just about every injury imaginable on the field. "What time?"

Traci stared at Billie. As she realized what "time" it was, Billie's eyes widened like they were an iPhone screen and two fingers ran across them in opposite directions. From the corner of her eye, Traci spotted the ref walking towards the sideline. She jumped to her feet and ran out on the field. Looking back over her shoulder, she yelled out, "Don't worry. I'm only hurt. I can still play Coach. Plus I took an Advil!"

Billie smiled and waved her on.

As the ball flipped end over end, Traci thought to herself *just eleven*. If she was in the Canadian Football League, she would have thought twelve. *Just eleven people between me and changing the world.* The ball landed in her hands and in that instant Traci only saw numbers.

Visions of all the great returns filled and left Traci's head as she swept to one side of the field. The tacklers followed. She counted down as each of the eleven reasons why she should not be able to make history became ten reasons when one of her blockers pushed a defender out of bounds. Nine reasons as another blocker took a defender off his feet. Eight reasons when a defensive player pulled a hamstring and fell.

And that's when Traci saw it. The hole form before the hole formed. She anticipated. She felt the future. She crossed the forty and could see the blocks being set up before they were set up. She turned on her jets and hit the hole. Each defender reached for her but was unable to even touch her. Just like in life, all the reasons why she couldn't succeed faded away in the midst of succeeding. Seven reasons. She was at the forty-five. Six reasons. Five reasons. Four reasons. She was at the fifty. Three reasons. Two reasons. Thirty yard line. One reason. If she failed, they would forever say there was only one reason the Lions didn't make it to the Super Bowl that year —a kicker.

It was fitting that all that stood in her way was the kicker. Either she could be great or he would be great. Traci aimed at him. They had called her a finesse player. Maybe that was true. Or *maybe* that was because she was a woman and that's what they wanted her to be... a finesse player. Maybe they ignored the times she built up enough speed, used all her skills as a martial artist and scientist to truck several players throughout the season. Today she was out for blood... humiliate the kicker. No one would be able to deny her legacy if she trucked a player on the road to the Super Bowl.

Traci dropped her shoulder and headed toward the kicker. The kicker moved from side to side but stopped when he noticed Traci move to match his movements. She was going to give him his shot. He stood at the twenty and she was giving him his shot. Twenty-five yard line. He set his feet. Twenty-four yard line. He opened his arms. Twenty-three yard line. He took a deep breath. Twenty-two. Twenty-one. He closed his eyes. He felt a light thump in the middle of his chest.

Cheers. He opened his eyes to see everyone standing. He had done it. The Colts were headed to the next round of the playoffs… Oh, what a feeling it was for those microseconds before he looked down on the ground and discovered Traci was not there. He could turn around but instead he decided to look up at the crowd and enjoy the applause. Then even that was interrupted as the replay appeared on the big screen.

That is just masterful control, Al. Mentally and physically. Emotions are high in a situation like this and sometimes you just want to run over everything. Why run over something when you can just as easily run around it.

And so it was that in one moment in time, Traci hesitated for a microsecond. Maybe if the kicker hadn't closed his eyes, he could have taken advantage of that moment and grabbed her. In that moment, Traci decided to spin more like Barry Sanders than run a muthafucka over like Marshawn Lynch. She playfully thumped the kicker on the chest as she *decided* she had nothing to prove. She always liked finesse players and was proud to be considered one. Besides, what if something went wrong? It would be much better to be a finesse running back with a Super Bowl ring than a power running back without one.

As the team carried her on their shoulders, she closed her eyes and sang, *"We out here drippin' in finesse…"* #BrunoMars

"Those who tell you to stick to sports are uncomfortable with our take on what we're seeing in the world and how it relates to sports."
– Cari Champion, Broadcast Journalist and ESPN Anchor

It was not easy being a thirteen-year old-kid on a mission. Especially when that thirteen-year-old kid had to go it alone. Shawn had more important things to do than take his son to every GameStop in and around "The D". That left Job with his trusty bicycle and the Detroit Public Transportation System, given that he hated ride shares because the drivers always wanted to start long conversations with him. By the second day, Job was a route expert.

Though technically his school suspension never happened, Job made the executive decision to extend his leave of absence because, like his father, he had more important things to do. Like figuring out how to unlock the game that protected the life he had built after losing so much. While he didn't think the team would trade anyone given the Lions' performance, who was to say that performance would continue with the PlayStation on the fritz. They could start to lose as badly as they won. *What if Cleo sold the team? A new owner could come in and clean the house. No!* For once, Job wanted to control his life and not be subject to the chaos inherent in a game of inches.

The principal didn't complain about Job's absence given he preferred not to have a brooding Job in his office every day. After reviewing several options, Job decided to go with strep throat since it would give him at least three free days and possibly four, if he called again with an extended fever.

The most obvious place to find Eli would be in the last place he had seen him. Isn't that what you do when you lose keys? Job had a sneaking suspicion that it wouldn't be that easy, and he was correct. It wasn't, so Job moved on to the next GameStop.

Over the next few days, Job's eyes were opened to a side of Detroit that he had only ever heard about but had never witnessed. He saw many vacant residences with boarded windows, and graffiti tattoos. He even saw houses that were so dilapidated that they could no longer be called houses, let alone homes. In his mind he classified them as structures. He saw kids, not much older than himself, roaming the streets in the middle of the day. He saw drug addicts passed out in once graveled lots that were slowly being swallowed by weeds.

His journey was not all plight and crime-ridden. He saw a lot of regular folks too with regular homes. In fact, he mostly saw regular folks and regular homes. One morning on the bus, he saw a father and his young daughter. From what he could gather from their conversation, the father worked nights but rode the bus every morning with his daughter to her school. The duo reminded him of Branson and Disney.

Job overheard a woman excitedly talking on her phone telling the person on the other end of the line she was on the way to the hospital to meet her first grand-baby. He thought about his grandmother and remembered that it had been a while since he had talked to her. One afternoon, an elderly gentleman sat across from Job with three bags of groceries in his lap. He reached inside one of the bags then pulled out a plastic container that was filled with cherries. "Nothing beats Michigan cherries. Do want a few?"

"Thanks," Job said, as he took a couple.

"Cherries are a superfood, you know. You start eating these now and you just might live forever."

Job chuckled. "Forever is a long time."

"Only when you're young."

Job saw many faces but not the one he was looking for. That changed on the third afternoon of his search. He was leaving a GameStop that was located in the Grandland Shopping Center. The crazy thing was that he did not notice Eli on his way inside the store, and Eli was not someone you would miss. Job walked over to where Eli was sitting on the concrete. Wearing a striped Baja hoodie and mala beads Eli resembled an aged hippie. "Have you been out here this whole time?"

"For a spell, I reckon," Eli answered. "How's the game been working for you?"

Job glanced up and saw a police vehicle slowly pass. He figured they had noticed Eli too and were trying to figure out what to make of him. "It *was* working great until it stopped working at all."

Eli looked up at the sky. Job's eyes followed suit, but he did not see anything other than a couple of birds perched on the overhead wires and a few fluffy white clouds.

"It can mean only one thing," Eli announced after an extended pause.

"Which is?"

Eli flashed a wide smile. "The game is finished. Congratulations."

"What... no!" Job shook his head with disgust. "The game isn't finished. You don't understand. We just started the playoffs. It can't be finished. I need *you* to fix it!"

Eli's bright smile turned sympathetic and kind. "No, it is you who do not understand. What's done is done. You cannot fix what ain't broken."

"Come on," Job's hand waved wide in frustration. "Don't try to finesse me with slick talk! Just tell me how to make it work again."

Job looked up and noticed a mother holding her young son's hand. He gave them an extra wide berth as they crossed the sidewalk. Across the street, he saw two men dressed in strange tattered clothing. They looked familiar. Just as Job opened his mouth to call to the tatteredly dressed men, he heard a deep voice speak from behind. "Excuse me, is this man giving you any trouble?"

Job turned around and saw the two police officers from the vehicle approaching them. "There isn't any trouble, Officer."

When Job turned, the men were gone and so was the mother. No, she was in the distance. But the men?

"What are you looking at? Look at me. Take your hand out of your pocket and slowly step away," the police officer commanded.

Job turned ready to defend Eli. "What are you..." Job mumbled as he looked down and saw that his hand was inside his pocket. The police officer was talking to *him*. "There isn't anything inside my pocket except an old receipt."

"Last warning," the second officer called out as he drew his pistol. "Step away."

Job complied and continued to speak. "We were just talking about a game," Job cried out with panic straining his voice.

A few seconds later, Job's face was squished against the concrete and his hands were handcuffed behind his back. The police officers then pulled him to his feet and began citing his rights as they searched his pockets.

After they were finished, the first police officer held out a small stash of cash in front of Job's face. "You mind explaining why there's four hundred dollars in your wallet?"

"You mean five hundred dollars!"

"Uh yeah, five hundred," the officer muttered.

"That's... that's my allowance." Job's voice trembled with fright. Tears stung his eyes until all he could see was the sight of a gun being pointed in his direction. Waiting for hot metal projectiles to stampede towards his little 14-year-old frame with one goal—to destroy him. Job wanted to do something—anything—to prevent it. But he was paralyzed with not one but many fears. Fear that Disney would weep so hard over his coffin that she would have no tears left for joy. Fear that his father would give up on life, decide that it was better to join Job beyond the sky. Fear that he might die or live but in a wheelchair. Fear that his name would join a list of other names so long that they would no longer fit on T-shirts, so numerous that one day mourners would have to swath themselves in blankets to commemorate the fallen.

"Allowance?" The police officers started to laugh. "Looks more like drug money to me."

Though time stood deadly still, Job's body began to quiver in terror. First his hands, then his arms. Before he knew it, a tremor spread throughout his body. He almost couldn't notice it over his pounding heart. And then the fear barreled back but differently. If he didn't stop shaking, maybe they would restrain him, choke him. At that moment, he simply didn't know what to do or not to do. He realized that there were six million ways to die and they only had to choose one.

"No," Job cried as he tried to whirl around but was held steady. He could see the news stories, posts, and headlines. He was about to be another Black person executed by a government employee tasked with his protection. *Six million ways to die, choose one.* In that moment he heard himself speak. "Please don't shoot me." *Four million ways..* "Please don't choke me." *Two million..* "Please don't kill me."

Job took several short deep panic filled breaths.

"I don't sell drugs. Ask him! Ask Eli! He will tell you. We were talking about a video game."

The police officers looked at Eli, who was once again pondering the sky with tranquil delight. "Is that true?"

"We were discussing many important things. For example, universal balance can only be achieved once we let go of things that no longer serve us… but to answer your question, no we were never talking about anything as simple as a video game."

"Alright then," the second police officer grunted. "We'll sort this out down at the station."

As he sat in the back of the cruiser, his breathing eventually slowed. His heart rate returned to normal. His body stopped shaking. He survived. Yet something was different. He didn't feel the same as he did this morning. Life. It was fleeting. He could be gotten too. Touched by, reached by, injured by forces beyond his control in a way that made everything he thought mattered seem trivial, petty and meaningless. Though he had survived the ordeal, something palpable had died inside of him.

...

In the span of less than two weeks, Shawn was called off the practice field once again because of his son. The only difference was that the first call had only caused mild panic compared to the second. As a parent, you have one job: protect your child from you, themselves, and the world. Every possible thing the world could do to his child, Shawn imagined it had happened. Just like he had failed to protect Day, he had now done the same with his son.

Maybe he had cursed his son the moment he chose the name Job. Day had balked at the name, because it meant "persecuted". It was Hebrew in origin and from the Old Testament, specifically the Book of Job. Job was a man whose faith was severely tested by God. Job had seven sons and three daughters. He owned seven thousand sheep, three thousand camels, five hundred yoke of oxen, and five hundred donkeys. In addition, Job had a large number of servants.

One day Satan and the Angels of God went to God. God bragged to Satan about his servant Job and how good he was. Satan said that the only reason why Job was good is because God was good to him and gave him sons, daughters, servants, and many animals. Satan asked if he could test Job. God gave him permission. However, God told Satan not to kill Job.

Satan put Job through a number of tests. First, Satan

took away all of Job's animals. Next, Satan killed the servants that were with the animals. Satan then killed all of Job's sons and daughters while they were eating together. Finally, Satan made Job sick. He afflicted sores over Job's entire body. Yet despite these tests, Job did not curse God like Satan wanted Job to do. He remained faithful.

Shawn focused on the patience and faith displayed by Job and not his trials. So in Shawn's mind, the name meant just that: patience and faith. The name was popular in the Netherlands, not so much in the USA. However, that didn't deter Shawn. If his son had faith in something and patience with everything else, the boy would be on the road to his best life.

Best life? This thought jarred Shawn's mind abruptly back to the reality of this moment. At this point, he would settle for a life. His imagination raced at warp speed through all the possible tragedies that could have befallen his precious baby boy. His body attempted to keep up with the velocity of the fear that coursed through his mind. Shawn's heart pumped faster, deeper, harder. His sweat glands began to flood his skin. And then his hands began to quiver. That quiver moved to his arms until it colonized his entire body.

Traffic! He smashed his horn as if it was nitrous. When it didn't clear a path he rode the shoulder like a private HOV lane, ticket be damned! Swerve! Shawn narrowly avoided a collision. He kept his foot to the floor. Brake! *Was that my exit?* He crossed the median to use the off-ramp. Horns sounded. His vision blurred. *Why couldn't he see?* What was this in his eyes all of a sudden? It had been so long since he had felt anything that he forgot the sight, taste, and smell of tears running down his face.

By the grace of angels, he arrived at the police station safe and sound and without causing any injury in his mad pursuit across the city. As he walked through the entrance to the station, he had one thought: whatever it was that Job had allegedly done. Theft? Assault? Murder? Job didn't do it. Shawn did it! Shawn would find a way to confess, to make himself out to be the perpetrator.

Shawn was greeted by police brass. Before any of them could utter a word, Shawn spoke with the presence of a father, resigned, determined and undeniable. "Take me to my son now." It may have been a world record in delivering a detainee. The brass looked on as Shawn and Job spoke. They were not lip readers but the hug he gave Job indicated that he was not interested in any other version of the story. He held his son's hand and walked out while eyeballing every person daring them to say something.

They were just minutes into their drive when Shawn received a call from the police station. All charges had been dropped. Now that he could relax, instead Shawn's fear magnified as the full gravity of the situation pressed down upon him. The drive back to their Bloomfield Hills estate was at a considerably slower pace but the tension that filled the Cadillac SUV was strong enough to set off a nuclear bomb. Eventually somewhere along the freeway, Shawn erupted. "So you're telling me you've been skipping school, riding all over Detroit to look for *Madden 19...*"

"I'm sorry..."

"Do... you have any idea what could have happened to you? *Do you?* What if that would have been some trigger-happy cop? You'd be dead. *You'd be dead.*"

Job's fist crashed upon the dashboard then he covered his face to hide the sobs that tore free from his throat. "I'm sorry... I'm sorry, Dad! I can't change that I'm Black."

Shawn pulled off along the side of the freeway and stopped the car. He wrapped his arms around his son, and pulled him close. Inside the huddle, they cried together.

*"In the absence of feedback, people will fill in the blanks with a negative.
They will assume you don't care about them or don't like them."*
~Pat Summitt, Head Coach, Tennessee Lady Volunteers

As soon as they got home, Job fled to his room. Shawn sat alone on a barstool beside the kitchen island and contemplated his next move. To date, his life could best be described as structured chaos. He was guided by strategies and protocols. Strategies and protocols he had chosen to ignore in the past, and he had suffered the consequences of these decisions. But he wasn't alone. Job had suffered too.

Job had attempted to pick up where his mother left off. But for Shawn, the grief of losing Day had changed him into something Job's mother wouldn't recognize. Job's childhood should have been filled with kid things: hanging out, shopping, and social media. Instead, he was forced into a world of adult things: buying groceries, paying staff, and paying bills.

A day would not pass without Shawn looking into Job's eyes and finding Day looking back at him. For a long time, he would see Day as he had in the last few moments they shared together on this earth. She had found him with another woman. It wasn't the first time, but it would be the last. She left the hotel room in a rage. Not even thirty minutes later, he received a call from the police. Day's SUV had rolled over. She was killed instantly.

Lately looking at Job, Shawn had started remembering the good times. Despite the ending and the roller-coaster ride in between, they did have some real good times. Shawn remembered the day they brought Job home from the hospital after he was born. Shawn had been terrified, but Day had handled everything like a pro. And their first Christmas together as a family, Shawn insisted on filling the entire living room with presents. They laughed hard when it was apparent that Job was more interested in the gift wrapping paper than the gifts.

But this afternoon when he looked at his son, he could not find a trace of Job's mother in his eyes. It scared him. Shawn wasn't much of a praying man, but he did not know what else to do. Nothing in his entire life had ever prepared him for the possibility that one day his son might be taken from him. *Day, baby, I know I'm the last person you want to hear from, but I need you. I need you real bad. I don't know what to do. I need you to show me what to do.*

Shawn nearly jumped out of his seat a few seconds later when his phone started to ring. He looked down and discovered that Traci was calling him.

"Shawn, I just saw the news. How is Job?"

It took Shawn a few moments to process her words. "The news?" He reached across the island for the remote, flipped on the television, and discovered Job was featured on *Sports Center*. A passerby had recorded the encounter between Job and the police officers on her phone and uploaded the video to YouTube, where it went viral within a few hours.

Folks, this isn't easy to watch. Earlier this afternoon, Job Lamb, son of Lions' Quarterback Shawn Lamb, was arrested and taken into custody by the Detroit Police. As most of you are aware, Shawn has a rather colorful history with the police. Is this an example of the apple not falling far from the tree, or is it yet another case of excessive police force? We have reached out to the Lions' organization, but both Cleo White, the owner, and Tip McMann, team President, have declined to comment.

Shawn sat speechless with his mouth agape in horror. He could not hear either the reporter or Traci on the other end of the line. All he could see was Job's face filled with terror and felt like he had been sucker punched straight in the gut.

"Shawn, I'm coming over," Traci rushed.

Shawn could not tear his eyes away from the screen. "K."

But Traci never heard the "K". She had already hung up and was on her way.

...

An hour later, Traci showed up with enough Chinese takeout to feed an offensive line. "I wasn't sure what y'all liked so I just ordered a little bit of everything. Where's Job?"

Shawn nodded upstairs and then stood silently in the corner and watched as Traci began unpacking the various containers.

"Well, don't just stand there. Go up there and tell your son it's time for dinner."

Traci let out a deep breath when he left the kitchen. She was not sure where that voice had come from. Maybe her mother? Whenever Traci had been sick or upset as a child, her mother turned into a little military sergeant. Through her mother, she learned that no matter what happens, you just keep going through the motions until those motions feel normal once again. Of course, at the time, her mother was nursing ear aches and heart breaks. Nothing that compared to this. Traci had no idea what to do in this situation, and she was sure Shawn felt equally helpless, but at least they had each other to figure it out.

Shawn and Job appeared a few moments later looking equally disgruntled, but Traci could see past their defenses. She waved them forward. "Come on, you both need something to eat."

Shawn trudged forward, but Job stood motionless. "I'm not hungry," he grumbled.

"Wonton soup it is. It's light on the stomach," Traci answered as she poured the soup in a bowl.

"Is it from that spot off 8 mile?" Shawn asked, trying to mute his emotions.

Truth be told, Traci did not think she could eat much either but that was not the point. Their world had just been shaken up like a gigantic snow globe. The sooner they found their way home the sooner they would be out of the soul-numbing frozen despair.

Once they were settled around the kitchen table, Traci quietly asked, "Do you want to talk about it?"

Job tucked his head low.

"You will need to eventually, and when you're ready, I will be there to listen," Traci said.

Job's stubborn chin lifted. Heat flashed in his eyes. "I didn't do anything wrong."

Traci reached for his hand. "There isn't a person on this planet, who knows the real you, that believes otherwise."

Job managed to swallow a couple spoonfuls of soup before he asked to be excused from the table. A few minutes later, Traci started to clean up.

Shawn took the plates from her hands. "You don't need to do that. You've done enough already."

Traci glanced around the kitchen with uncertainty both at the mess and also silently wondering if she overstepped her bounds.

"I mean it, Traci. From the bottom of my heart, *thank you*. I don't know what I would have done without you tonight. I've never been this scared in my life."

Traci felt her face burning with embarrassment. "You will figure it out."

"I hope so... I sure do hope so."

As Shawn was walking Traci to her car, another vehicle

pulled into his drive. At first, he wondered how this person had gotten past the guards, then he wondered if it might be Cleo because he could not make out the driver in the dark. Much to his surprise, he discovered it was Tip.

Traci's eyes widened with concern. "Do you need me to stick around?"

"Nah," Shawn denied. "I've got this. It's getting late. I'll see you tomorrow."

Tip exited his vehicle looking tired, disheveled, and as un-Tip as Shawn had ever seen. He stopped and waved at Traci as she backed out and then wearily climbed the front steps of Shawn's porch. "I'm sorry. I know I shouldn't be here. But I just had to know—how's Job?"

Shawn's player mode activated. He started to smile like he was in front of the camera but a wave of exhaustion crashed across his soul. "He's scared, Tip. Real scared."

Tip shook his head in disgust. Temporarily at a loss for words, his mouth opened and then closed again. *Maybe he had used up all his words charming the guards*? Driving over to Shawn's house had been more of a compulsion than impulse. He had no intention of stopping, but here he was and now he did not know what to say. Only that was not really true. He knew what he wanted to say, needed to say, but he did not know what on heaven's earth possessed him with this uncontrollable urge to say it. "I want to apologize."

Shawn blinked with surprise. "Why?"

"I don't know," Tip gasped. "I don't know why I need to apologize to you for what happened. I only know that I do."

"I'm…" Shawn stepped back. "I'm not sure what to say."

Tip nodded. "Just know if you or your son ever need anything, anything at all, call me. The Lions' organization supports *you both* one hundred percent."

...

Job knew that his dad would come in to check on him before he went to bed, so he was not surprised when his door opened. But he was shocked to discover that Shawn was carrying a sleeping bag and a pillow. Job sat up in his bed. "What are you doing?"

"After your mama died, you used to have real bad nightmares, so every night I would sleep on your floor. You probably don't remember that."

Job did, but he was not willing to admit it. "Dad… I'm not a kid anymore."

"Good thing," Shawn said as he unrolled the sleeping bag and placed it on the floor at the end of Job's bed. He fluffed the pillow and settled inside the bag. "Because I ain't sleeping down here for you. If you hear any hollers or whimpers, just give me a good nudge. That'll be enough to make the terror pass."

They both laughed.

Every morning, the mirror told Branson a truth that he tried to ignore for the rest of the day. No matter how good he felt about his life, it had not been paid for by his labor but by the pain of someone else. Whatever power he thought he now possessed had already been usurped by Tip before Branson had a chance to put it to work.

He had a mission. A mission that if successfully completed would all but erase the most disgraceful thing he had ever done: hurting a woman for being a woman. But today, Branson entered Tip's office as a new man. He was living his truth, playing the game he loved at the highest level, and he was determined to get his power back.

People plan, God laughs, but only Luck gets the joke. Today Branson got the joke. As Branson crossed the doorway, a sight that would cancel his courage with a hashtag had no effect on him. Tracy stood slightly behind a seated Tip, as if posing for their super villain Hall of Fame portraits. Branson was ready. In part because he had followed his daughter's advice, "Stay ready so you don't have to get ready, dad." And so he was and his voice rang like a guy who knew it, "Tip, Tracy."

"Branson, my guy," Tracy bellowed as he moved forward to give Branson a man hug. Branson silently glared at Tracy like a lion trying to decide if something was prey or predator. Tracy took the hint and stayed in place. Branson breathed a mental sigh of relief. Branson didn't want to touch Tracy, DAYUM sure didn't want to hug him. For Branson was wearing a recording device Billie had given him for the meeting.

Branson took a seat in front of Tip's desk. In order to get them to talk, Branson knew he had to become prey at some point, and appear non-threatening. "So am I being traded?" Branson asked.

"Traded!? Noooo! Branson, we just wanted to connect with you. Make sure you're ok after everything that happened."

"I don't want to talk about it," Branson spat as he rose from his chair and headed toward the door. He didn't rush, he moved deliberately.

"Wait, don't leave, Branson!" Tip said with a bit of desperation. Maybe Tip was starting to like this new Lions' organization. Maybe it was the winning. Maybe it was all the goodwill the team was receiving. Or maybe it was the profits. Either way, Tip needed to make sure Branson was copacetic.

"Tip, I just want to forget about it."

Branson peeked his head through the doorway and looked back and forth. He dipped back in and closed the door. He donned his best wide-eyed frightened look and began to approach Tip and Tracy.

"I take no pride in allowing you to blackmail me by threatening to expose that I'm gay. I take no pride in Tracy being your messenger, button-man. Giving me the cloak-and-dagger head nod to hurt that woman, your fiancé, little Traci. I knew and both of you knew that if I missed a block in that game, she was going to get laid out. Hell, it could be a crime, so excuse me if I don't want to implicate myself by having this discussion."

Tip and Tracy stared at Branson. They each weighed his

words and thought how best to proceed. Tracy reasoned that they had what they wanted. But Tip wanted to close the deal and figured empathy was the best way to go.

"Branson, you're right. I'm sorry for doing that to you. We are sorry, aren't we, Tracy?"

Tracy stared at Branson for a few uncomfortably long seconds. He twisted his lips and mouth from left to right as he pondered if he should make peace. Without any desire to even fake sincerity, he said, "Yeah, we're sorry."

Tracy extended his hand and moved towards Branson. He had the confession he needed, so Branson backed away and quickly searched for a reason to turn down Tracy's mea culpa.

"I'm not there yet. It's enough for me that we don't discuss it anymore."

Tracy put his hand up, as if a robber had entered the room, and took a few steps backwards.

"On that note, I have an interview so I'm going to go."

Branson turned around and headed towards the door. Before he could exit, Tip asked one last question that would help him sleep at night.

"Branson, you aren't recording this?"

Branson kept walking, opened the door and didn't look back, "Come, Tip, you know Michigan is a two-party state."

"Of course."

Branson exited just as Tip answered. Tracy's brow wrinkled.

"You know Michigan is a one-party state, right? Only one party needs to give consent to record a conversation."

Tip stared at the door as it slowly closed.

"Yes, Tracy, I know."

"Doug, it's obvious you've been a black quarterback all your life. When did it start to matter?"
~Butch John, Sports Journalist, Orlando Sentinel

Disney dodged and swayed through the crowded school hallway with her backpack tucked close to her belly. Looking very much like her father, she yelled out, "Job, wait up!" She was breathless by the time she caught up to him. "Was that your dad I saw out front?"

Scarcely slowing his pace, Job tucked his head. "Yeah...I don't want to talk about it."

Disney reached for his arm to stop him. "What don't you want to talk about? Your dad bringing you to school? Or the fact that you were arrested yesterday? I *saw* you on the news last night. I tried to call you..."

"I know, Disney." Job shrugged out of her reach and marched in silence towards his locker.

Disney trailed behind him all too aware of the looks the other students were giving them. Over the past week, she had grown accustomed to the unsolicited attention, but the extra wide berth thing was new. She did not know if they were outcasts because the other students thought they were contagious or because they were scared. Disney had never imagined there would be such a fine line between untouchable and hero.

Job rummaged through his locker. Loose papers, pens, devices, chargers, and old headphones scattered to-and-fro. Not so long ago, his locker would have been immaculately organized, but that was before the game had taken over his life. "We were having an inner circle moment," he mumbled as he reached for his algebra textbook.

"I thought I *was* a part of your inner circle."

Job shook his head in disgust. "What do you want me to say, Disney? You were right. We never should have played that game."

Disney looked on helplessly as Job slammed his locker shut and walked away. She did not approach him again until lunchtime.

...

Disney found Job sitting alone in the cafeteria. She kind of figured she would find him this way. What did surprise her was that the tables surrounding him were also vacant. A few students standing along the perimeter glanced in his direction but none of them were brave enough to approach. With her tray in hand, Disney confidently maneuvered through the throng and placed her lunch down in front of him. "What's the matter with you? You've got BO or something?"

Job glared at Disney.

Disney sat down. Her eyes passed over the California medley with disinterest. No matter how green the broccoli, orange the carrots, and white the cauliflower were, no thirteen-year-old in their right mind would choose that over pizza. She held up the slice of pepperoni pizza and said, "This was an unexpected treat. It's not even Friday."

Job's lunch tray remained untouched. "My dad bought it."

"Your dad bought pizza for the entire school? Nice."

Job shrugged. "Maybe… I guess."

Disney took a bite of the pizza. "It's really not that bad."

"The pizza?"

Disney flashed a wide smile. "That too, but actually I was talking about the game."

Job leaned back in his chair and crossed his arms in front of his chest. His head cocked to one side. "How can you even say that? Your parents are getting divorced!"

"True," Disney agreed between bites of pizza. Once she was finished, she started eyeing the uneaten slice on Job's tray. "But, I've never seen either of my parents this happy. I don't know…" she shrugged, "maybe they are just putting on a front for my benefit? Dad found a new home. It's two houses down the road from ours, and he and Mom have already started shopping for furniture. She is going to decorate it for him."

"Sounds confusing to me."

"It is, but I would rather see them behaving like confusing friends than logical enemies. A few weeks ago, the life I knew was over, but it turns out it just needed to be resorted. I bet you'll find the same too."

"Disney, I had a gun drawn on me. I know you're trying to find the silver lining in every situation, but sometimes there just isn't one to be found."

"But now you can say it. Well, if someone ever points a gun at you and you don't flinch."

"Say what, Disney?"

"You can stare at them and say, forgive me for being underwhelmed, but this isn't the first time I've had a gun pointed in my face," Disney said with a goofy grin.

Job shook his head and buried his face in his food. Disney looked at Job's reflection in his phone that lay face up next to his plate. A slight smirk crossed his face.

...

The next five weeks were grueling. Despite their victories, there was not a single member of the Lions' team or staff that was not physically and mentally exhausted. Without fail, every time patience was stretched thin and tempers began to flare, Cleo would magically appear on the practice field with homemade baked treats. Billie would give Cleo the frowning of her life. However, this subsided as it was hard to stay angry when your mouth was stuffed with fresh-from-the-oven chocolate chip cookies. Still, Billie shooed her from the field as soon as she finished her cookie.

It was during one of those breaks that Cleo asked to speak to Shawn in private while Billie was rallying the troops. "I've been asked to speak about Job's altercation. I haven't because I didn't feel that it was my place. I just wanted to be sure that you did not misunderstand the reason for my silence, and I hope you realize that you have the full support of the Lions' organization. If you want me to state my opinion, I would be more than willing to share it."

Shawn looked at the players as they watched Billie. There may have been some resistance in the beginning, but now there wasn't a player among them who would not be willing to march alongside her into the harshest battle.

"Thanks. It wasn't an altercation but a profiling."

Cleo nodded in agreement, "Yes, profiling!"

"That means a lot, but right now I've got to focus on healing my son. When the time is right, I'll say what needs to be said."

Cleo nodded in agreement. "It's your call, Shawn."

Shawn stuck to his guns despite the pressure he received from the media to address *the situation*. Every time he heard those two words uttered together, Shawn knew he was doing the right thing. Job was not *the situation*. Job was his son.

Traci was the one who suggested counseling. Admittedly, Shawn wanted no part of it for either of them. He didn't need a *professional* to tell him what to do for his son. Or so he thought. But late one night when he could not sleep, Shawn was googling and stumbled across some medical terms like post-traumatic stress disorder. Shawn had heard of PTSD but thought it was just something soldiers brought home from the war. He was stunned when he discovered that it was actually very common, that it could happen to any person after experiencing a terrifying event, and could lead to depression, anxiety, and self-destructive behaviors. They started family counseling the very next day.

As much as Shawn wanted counseling to be a magic cure, it wasn't. Certain events are life-defining and split your timeline into two: who you were before something happened, and who you are after. The terror Shawn felt when he saw the video for the first time would always be a part of him, just like Job's trauma would always be with him. He hoped they both could learn to tame the fear and mold it into something constructive.

To do that, he needed the right person beside him. As much as he had come to admire and respect both Billie and Cleo, to do what he wanted to do, Shawn needed someone else by his side. Someone connected. Someone that spoke the language of the oppressor. Someone that looked like the oppressor. Cause that was the way of the oppressor. So when the time was right, he called in the favor.

...

Two days before the big game, Shawn and Tip held a much anticipated joint press conference. Shawn started by placing a box of tissues on the table between them. "Y'all know I'm about to get emotional talking about my only child."

The reporters sat poised on the edge of their seats. A muted chuckle ricocheted across the room. Shawn glanced back behind the screen where Job was standing with Traci.

"A few weeks ago, my son, Job, made a poor decision. He decided to skip school because he wanted to purchase a video game. Back in my day, I skipped school a couple times. Whenever I was caught, my mother would whoop my... whack me with a switch and ground me..." Shawn's words fell short. The room began to blur behind the tears that filled his eyes. "...but never once... not a single time did I have a gun drawn on me, my face smashed against the concrete. Not once was I placed in handcuffs—because I *skipped school.*"

Shawn silently shook his head as he reached for a tissue. "I can't even begin to describe the fear I felt as a parent watching those things happen to my son. Short of losing your child, there's nothing to compare to that... watching helplessly and realizing how close I came to having my only child taken away from me. If you've never felt that feeling, then before you go to sleep tonight, get down on your hands and knees and pray that you don't ever have to know what it feels like. Job's a real good kid. A really good kid! He didn't deserve that and neither does any other person in this country. But I didn't ask you here today to play the blame game. I can't lie. I'm happy that the officers involved were fired. Given the fact that both were involved in similar incidents while employed as officers in other states only makes me even more elated. That said, I want to start a dialogue and try to figure out some sort of way so that no parent has to go through this again. A government should not accost, harass and persecute its citizens!"

Shawn paused and Tip leaned forward into his microphone. "I hate to correct you on national television, but Shawn you are mistaken. Job isn't a good kid—he's a truly phenomenal kid."

Shawn nodded and managed a half-grin even though his heart was heavy.

"Look, folks, I'm an old white man. Sitting beside me is a not-as-old African-American man..."

"Hey now," Shawn interjected.

Tip chuckled as he looked over at Shawn. "I would

have said young man, but you aren't a spring chicken anymore. I reckon we've known each other for going on three years now."

"That sounds about right."

"And, it's safe to say that we've had our fair share of lively debates."

Shawn chuckled. "True."

Tip looked back at the reporters sitting in front of him. "The two of us could probably go at it right here, and no one in this room would think anything about it... but what if we were having one of our debates somewhere off the field or podium? What if we were someplace where no one knew either of us? Would assumptions about who is right and who is wrong be made? Would Shawn be arrested simply because of the color of his skin? We live in a world where we see things, but it never hits home until it happens to someone you know. When I saw that video, I was shaken to my core because I know Job. He is kind and caring, and honestly, if I ever had a son, I couldn't think of a better role model than Job. This has to stop, folks! When I watched that video, I knew that I wanted to use whatever little power and influence I have to make this stop, but I didn't know how until a few days ago when Shawn called me."

Shawn propped his hands on the table and leaned forward into his microphone.

"I know a lot of people out there have been praying for my family, and I want to say thank you. We are doing all we can to heal and move past this. Since that day, I've been giving a lot of thought about what I want to say and what I need to do next—I realized that we can never be completely healed until everyone is healed. With that in mind, Cleo, Tip, and I have agreed that it is time for a change. To that end, the Lions' organization will donate $50 million dollars to commence a study, initiate lobbying efforts to determine the viability and seek to affect the introduction of a bill to prevent the employment of any officer that has been involved in a questionable act of violence against American citizens even where the officer is acquitted in the court of law. We want to prevent police force hopping by officers throughout the country. You may find work somewhere in the universe but not here in the State of Michigan, not in the United States of America."

"For one, when has Jay-Z ever taken a knee to come out and tell us that we're past kneeling? Yes, he's done a lot of great work, a lot of great social justice work. But for you to get paid to go into an NFL press conference and say that we're past kneeling? Again, asinine."
~Eric Reid, Activist, Safety, Carolina Panthers

I do believe this is the second time that a Super Bowl has been played in the home town of one of the participating teams.

Job sat in the owner's box with Disney. Cleo sat at one end and Tip on the other. All those weeks of saying *just one more time* had come down to this final moment. A bone weary exhaustion descended upon them, squelching any lingering remnants of elation. Strain filled their faces as each silently considered the price of victory.

Michaels' voice echoed from the speakers. *Yeah, Detroit definitely has the home field advantage, but will that be enough is the question everyone is asking. I've got to say, going into the playoffs, the Lions were hands down everyone's favorite to win, but these past couple of weeks we have seen an entirely different team.*

Madden answered. *That's true, but I think we can all agree that win or lose this season, the Lions have irrevocably changed the face of the NFL.*

The Lions won the coin toss and opted to receive in the second half. The defense took the field, but it was short-lived because the Raiders' offense was virtually unstoppable. Within the first minute of the game, Las Vegas put seven on the board via a deep pass on second down.

Once again, Madden's voice could be heard inside the owner's box. *This doesn't look promising.*

Job sank low in his seat. Disney covered her face with her hands. Cleo softly chuckled. "Ye of little faith."

First in ten, back on the field, Shawn saw the ref raise his arms over his head. Then what felt like only a second later, a flag was thrown.

Delay of game. Five yard penalty. Offense.

"It's okay… it's okay," Shawn grunted to rally the troops.

The second down was more promising. The Lions gained five yards. Traci looked towards the sideline where the punter was stretching his leg. "Not yet."

Third time's the charm, or so Shawn thought. Traci was bogged down by the defense. No one else was open either. Shawn tucked the ball and ran down the field. At ten yards to the goal line, the ball slipped out of his grasp. Stunned, Shawn pivoted on his heel just in time to see it recovered by the defense that ran it all the way back to the other goal line.

The rest of the first half was just as dismal. Shawn was sacked. Branson fumbled— multiple times. The only highlight of the game for Disney and Job thus far was when two power couples, entered the box. All the nervous chatter stopped the instant they walked through the door. The hushing of the crowd extended even to Cleo as Tip silently noted that even "Little Miss Activist" recognized the celebrity duo.

"Job, don't look," Disney said through her teeth.

Job immediately turned, looked, and started talking through his teeth, "Why are we talking through our teeth?"

"I told you not to look!"

"Ok, I'm not looking."

"It's Beyoncé and her husband."

"You mean Jay-Z?" Job said with a furrowed brow.

"Like I said Beyoncé and her husband."

"You and Jay-Z got beef?"

Disney twisted her lips in the affirmative. Job took a deep breath.

"Let me guess? You feel like he be hanging with the ops? You don't like that he was cutting deals with the NFL trying to be an owner when Colin still didn't have a job?

Disney shook her head no.

"That he said he talked to Kap about it and then Kap came out and was like no he didn't?"

Disney shook her head no. Job started to speak but Disney interrupted him.

"And before you ask, no it wasn't the fact that while Jay-Z was running around saying, 'We got all we can out of kneeling' the NFL's official policy regarding paying brain injury settlement claims for their players was that Black people are not as smart as white people, so Black people should get paid less or have their claims denied."

Job started to speak but Disney interrupted him.

"And it's not because all this was happening while the NFL was running around publicly apologizing for not listening to Kaepernick sooner."

Job took a breath and started to speak but Disney interrupted him... again.

"And it's not because when Black people attempted to point out back in the 90s that this racial normalization policy, i.e. comparing test scores among economically and culturally similarly situated people would help equalize the playing field because standardized tests are biased and rich people tend to do better than poorer people on said standardized tests, conservatives said hell no. We should compare apples to apples because otherwise aren't we rewarding beneficiaries of white supremacist policies?"

Job took a breath and started to speak but Disney interrupted him... once again.

"And it's not because the conservatives that made so much noise in opposition to racial normalizing when it would have been used to help Black people were so quiet when it was used against Black people that you could hear a rat piss on cotton."

Job chuckled. Disney glared at him. Job waited a moment to see if Disney would interrupt him again. Job started to speak but then Disney...well you know.

"Black players start out with lower cognitive function. The fuck." Disney mumbled in anger.

"They should be ashamed of themselves. Standardized tests are not a valid indicator of intelligence. Especially in football where all they care about is the cognitive function to run, kick, catch, throw, and hit," Job said.

Disney nodded in agreement.

"Well, that ain't really Jay-Z's fault. It's just generally fucked up. But you need to be careful before you go singing kumbaya when you just don't know enough about who you holding hands with."

Disney nodded in agreement.

"Hmmmm. So if it will benefit Black people, it's a hell no but if it is a determinant to Black people, it's a hell yeah."

"Right."

Disney and Job stared at Beyoncé and Jay-Z.

"So why you mad at Jay-Z again? It had to be about Kap."

"That's the problem, it wasn't about Jay-Z. Though I'm happy he became the owner of the Giants. Our support of Kap's problem wasn't about Jay-Z becoming an owner. But our support of Kap and Eric, anyone coming after them, was about making sure that when anyone spoke the truth, that they didn't have to worry about being blackballed. But that's not why we got beef."

Job nodded.

"Sooooo why you mad?"

"Cause his aura is in close proximity to B's. So I don't want his bullshit spilling over and fuckin' with Beyoncé's perfect reputation."

"Perfect? So Beyoncé can do no wrong?"

"Rule one: Beyoncé don't do nothing wrong. Rule two: if you believe that Beyoncé has done something wrong, check Rule one."

They both laugh.

"So Beyoncé is perfect.'

"Yes."

"Ok so if Beyoncé came over here right now. Used all the strength of her Beyoncéness to pick me up and throw me onto the field and kill me, would she still be perfect in your eyes?"

Disney stared at Job.

"Honestly? Yes, she would still be perfect."

"What?"

"I would be like yeah throw that little muthafucka B!"

"You wouldn't even ask why?" Job asked in fake shock.

"No cause you obviously did something and though I don't know what it is, Beyoncé does and she is looking out for me!"

They both burst into hysterical laughter. Disney stopped laughing and turned stone-faced.

"Job, don't look," Disney said.

Job immediately turned, looked, and started talking through his teeth, "Why are we talking through our teeth again?"

"So when I tell you 'don't look', you hear 'look', huh?"

"Ok, I'm not looking this time. I'm side-eyeing."

Disney rolled her eyes.

"It's the Obamas!"

Job's head swung like it was on a swivel, "I'm saying something."

Disney clinched her hands, and said, "Don't!"

Job noticed her entire body tighten, and said, "Ok relax."

Disney complied and relaxed.

Job waved, "Barack!"

Disney covered her face and turned away, mortified.

Barack walked over to Job and held out his hand. "Look man, I just wanted to say that what you and your pops are doing is important for the culture and America. It's necessary. We should talk."

Job's eyes were huge as he reached for Barack's outstretched hand. "Thanks," he managed to mumble.

Barack nodded towards Disney; she refused to turn her head.

Michelle joined Barack and grabbed his hand. Job smiled at her, "Can you give me a tip? Some life advice. A jewel?" Job didn't know where the question came from but something told him to ask her. Barack laughed.

"You got any jewels, Michelle?"

Michelle smiled at Job, "With the right person by your side, the sky's the limit. We have to head back down for the show, but it was a real honor meeting you."

Job looked dazed. "Same to you."

Unable to contain herself, Disney jumped out of her seat and wrapped her arms around Michelle. "I love you," she whispered with her head resting against the sequined costume.

"Awww," Michelle sighed. "What's your name, sweetheart?"

Disney leaned back so she could look at her idol in the eyes. "My name is Disney."

"Thank you, Disney! I don't know which is more beautiful, you, your spirit or your name." Michelle squeezed her close for one last hug. Just as she finished, Beyoncé sans Jay-Z came over. Unable to contain herself, Disney hugged Beyoncé and professed her undying devotion.

When Barack, Michelle, and Beyoncé left, they took their stardust with them and reality crashed the party. By the end of the second quarter, there was not anyone sitting in the owner's box who still believed that the Lions had a chance of winning. The only hope left now was that it would not be a complete shutout.

Michaels echoed their thoughts. *Here we are at the half and it is clearly one of the most one-sided Super Bowls ever played. Las Vegas leads forty-two to zero.*

Cleo and Tip slipped away to talk with the other adults in the box. Tears slipped down Disney's cheeks. "I didn't think it would feel like this. My dad just seems…I mean did he have to throw so many picks."

Job watched as the field was being converted into a stage. "You ever see the movie *Philadelphia* with Tom Hanks? My mom loved it. She would watch it over-and-over and always cried at the end. My dad loves *Rocky* and still cries when Apollo dies. I never could understand why they would torture themselves like that, but my mom told me that whenever they watched those movies, they would get caught up in the movie like they were watching it for the first time and hoped that something was going to change."

"So you think I feel this way because I believed they had a chance to win?"

"Maybe," Job answered. "And, I guess nothing is impossible."

Disney snorted. "You don't sound convinced."

Inside the locker room, Billie stood in front of her team.

"There isn't a person in this room who hasn't fought some sort of battle this season. Some fought publicly and some fought in private. And what I'm about to ask you, well, just isn't right. You've already given your all, but now I'm asking for more. Now is the time, lady and gentlemen. You've got to dig past your limits. You have to give more than you have."

Shawn stood up. "Coach, do you mind if I say a few words?"

Billie stepped back and stood with Stan.

"Standing out there on the field in our pads and uniforms, it's real easy to forget that this isn't just a game. We've all been called to fight a bigger battle. We ain't just fighting for some trophy. Today we fight for every little girl out there who dreams of one day playing for the NFL. Today we fight for every single person who is made to feel ashamed because of who they love. Today we fight for anyone that has a dream that they don't want deferred. Today we fight for our families. Our friends. Our city. Ourselves. Today we are going to show them what happens when a pride of lions decides enough is enough. We are going to give it all and more. Because they believe in us."

The team leaped to their feet and roared.

Back inside the owner's box, Madden could be heard saying—*I'm not sure what happened during halftime but this looks like an entirely different team.*

Job remained doubtful until first down. Shawn handed the ball to Traci. Branson smashed two defenders knocking them to the ground. The field opened up and Traci ran eighty yards for the touchdown. While Branson and Traci celebrated in the end zone, Shawn looked up at the owner's box and waved. Job knew right then and there that his father didn't need a mystical video game as he had found his own magic.

Over the next two quarters, the Lions fought hard and steady, chipping away at the lead with each play. Time ticked away. Fourth down, 40 yards out, down five, and only ten-seconds remaining on the play clock, from inside the huddle, Shawn waited for the call to be transmitted into his helmet from the sideline. Tension in sport is like a time dilation device that makes every second feel like an hour of anxiety.

Powerless. That's how football fans felt in these situations. They didn't play. Fans couldn't block, run, or throw and directly determine the outcome. At best, they could channel their emotions into sonic and visual psychic energy, hype for their chosen warriors. It was representative democracy at its finest. Though it was never proven scientifically, it was well established that teams played better at home than on the road. Homefield advantage was a thing, and the fans had everything to do with that thing.

For Lions' fans, who had never won a Super Bowl or even appeared in a Super Bowl, it was worse. The thought that they could win their first Super Bowl at home was almost too much for a human—even one from Detroit—to handle. Their stomachs churned, their palms sweat, their bodies buzzed with chills, their lungs burned from panic breaths, their eyes teared, and their minds both fatalized and optimized the outcome at the same time. If losing was death and winning was life, they saw themselves living and dying ad infinitum.

And wealth and fame wasn't a magic elixir for the symptoms. The mood in the suites and the owner's box was the same. Even Tip, who had tried to sabotage it all, after years of being an executive of a Super Bowless franchise and Super Bowl appearance-less franchise, found that Tums were needed. This could be his crowning achievement.

Cleo, though she had once upon a time given less than a damn about sports, closed her eyes in mediation. The emotions she felt bubbling were familiar. Nervous, excited, frightened in a good way all at the same time. Falling and flying, love.

The sidelines were not spared. After all the back and forth and adrenaline had subsided regarding what play to call, they were left with the same vehemence that plagued the fans in seats and boxes alike. Powerless.

Shawn heard the call. Pass. Pass to the wideout. He shook his head. Sure it was the right football play. He would be the tallest thing in the endzone, a spontaneous sprouted redwood. It would give every player with an ego, a true competitor, what they had always wanted. It would give that player—the one that if you opened their head all you would find is a football—what they wanted: the ball in their hand when the game was on the line, the ball in their hand.

Shawn wasn't your typical true competitor. He had lost his football ego long ago. If you opened Shawn's head, you would find a football but not just a football. You would find a wide variety of interests, thoughts on things outside of football. You would find passion for art, music, and fashion. You would find activism, consciousness, and desire for justice. You would find love for family, friends, and the game, love for the bigger game. And that is why Shawn called an audible and rather than the right football play, "Traci, you've got to run like the wind... and Branson don't let anyone near her."

Branson's heart dropped and popped back in place. He knew that this was a chance to make his amends to Traci more perfect. Sure, he had said sorry. Sure, he had worked with Billie to secure Traci's equity. Sure he had done all he could, but like his game, there was always something more that could be done. Branson knew he could never be perfect at anything, but he could always do better. He wouldn't annoy Traci by apologizing through words, instead he would apologize through action. She placed her hand on his shoulder and he knew she trusted him to protect her for the next few minutes, possibly the most crucial minutes of her life.

Traci didn't move her hand from the huddle. She kept her hand there a second longer than socially acceptable, and she felt a calm energy leaving Branson's body and entering hers. Today she needed calm, because for some reason, she hadn't felt herself. What hadn't changed was the pressure. The knot that she had felt the first time Shawn tossed her the ball would soon be back. Except this time it wouldn't be accompanied with doubts. There would be no questions about her abilities, why she was here and if she could do it, she already had done it. This time it would cement her, the team, and a new day in history. Regardless of the importance of the next play, what she really wanted was just to feel the ball in her hands. She wanted to play football.

The offense assumed a five WR set. The ball was hiked. They headed for the endzone. Shawn faked a hand-off to Traci. No one bit. The Lions offense save three offensive linemen shot towards the end zone. Raiders rushed four but the three lineman held them off long enough for Shawn to throw what looked to be a Hail Mary that had no chance to reach the endzone.

Five...four...three... The most missed shot in basketball is what many consider the easiest, the layup. While everyone else was 15 yards ahead of her, Traci circled back to make a layup and hoped no defender was close enough to knock her into next week. She knew a hit could have come at any moment but she had to concentrate on the catch.

Traci pivoted on her heels with her hands stretched towards the sky. Before she knew it the ball lay securely in her hands, a cub she needed to carry the den. The crowd let out a collective gasp as they realized it was a trick play. Most of the defense had followed most of the team to the endzone and the remaining were behind her. Branson didn't go to the endzone and had just enough time to build up a bit of momentum to knock down one LB that got a bead on Traci.

It created a micro-sized hole, a nano window of opportunity, but it would have to do. Traci turned on her jets and she was almost at the ten before she encountered opposition. The rest of the pride had cleared them out. *No holding... no holding. No penalties y'all.* A LB launched his frame at Traci, side step hop. Another DB tried to tackle her up high, stiff arm! Two defenders left, with space between.

They came at her, almost simultaneously. Bam! She caught one with her shoulder at just the right moment and he fell to the ground. One more to beat. He grabbed Traci up high and attempted to drag her down. Traci shook him off. Only five yards to go. *Ugh!* All of a sudden it felt like she was walking in quicksand. At the same time, the crowd erupted. Traci looked down as she was inches from the goal line. She saw two defenders desperately holding onto her legs and feet. Traci had dragged them to the endzone. She was at the goal line and two more defenders had recovered and were headed towards her. She stuck out the football to touch the pylon. Like a bam-bam play she was popped by a defender that launched himself. Traci fell to the ground but she was not in the endzone.

Silence. The referee ran from the sideline with arms in the air signaling touchdown. At the same time, a yellow flag flew onto the field. The referees all congregated.

There appears to be a flag on the field. Al observed.

Not just any flag but a game deciding flag. If it's on the offense then that could mean they replay the down but with the offense further back. And it's not likely that the Raiders will fall for a trick play twice. If it's on the defense then the Lions' are Super Bowl champs. But that is assuming Traci broke the plane and the ref saw it!

What do you think the call is?

It could be holding Al as you could call that on every play. Madden replied.

The refs broke their huddle.

Looks like the refs are ready.

The lead ref faced the crowd and adjusted his mic, "There is a flag on the play,"

The ref paused for dramatic effect.

Job shouted, "Oh he's finessin' this moment for all he can!"

"Facts!" Disney concurred.

The ref continued, "Against the defense for unnecessary roughness for a helmet to helmet hit."

The crowd took a collective deep breath, prepared to release it as a sad rumble or victorious lion's roar. All depended on the words the ref spoke next.

"That penalty is declined, the runner made contact with the pylon before being downed, and the ruling on the field is a TOUCHDOWN!" The ref launched his hands straight up in the air to indicate touchdown.

The stadium exploded with shouts and applause. Job reached for Disney and whirled her around in circles. Cleo stood speechless for several seconds before she joined in the joviality.

Tip stood back and after a moment, he reached into his pocket for a tissue to wipe his eyes. Maybe it was the moment that had made him cry. Overwhelmed by the realization of a goal that he had worked for all of his life. Or maybe it was the police officer that waited incautiously in the corner to escort Tip a few blocks over to answer questions about a tape that implicated him and another as yet unidentified man in a conspiracy to commit extortion and fraud.

People like Tip, those that were friends with the assistant police chiefs, weren't arrested but invited to the station. Before he went on what might be a 20-year excursion with a $10,000 price tag not including attorney fees, he needed to clear his conscience. Though it wasn't a confession booth, the field would have to do.

Tip made his way from the box to the field. He flashed his all access pass and pointed at the officer to alert the stadium personnel that the officer was with him. Tip saw Tracy first and gave a wave. Tracy waved back and started to approach but saw the police officer close enough to Tip and thought better of it. Sure, there were police everywhere but something about Tip and this officer didn't feel... right. Plus there was a celebration to be had.

Tip scanned the crowd and saw who he was looking for. It took a bob-and-weave to box his way through the crowd to reach his destination. Once he did, Traci turned around and Tip didn't know what to say. As he searched for words, Shawn walked to Traci's four o'clock. Not enough to interfere but just enough to let her know he was there. Branson noticed and walked to Traci's six.

Given that he had publicly harmed her, he saw no need for his groveling to be private. Tip leaned into Traci's ear and said, "I'm sorry. What I did was beyond wrong. I tried to hold you back for no other reason than what parts you had. It was cowardly and I need to do a lot of work on myself. When I do, I will ask for forgiveness. For now, thank you for hearing me out."

Maybe it was the fact that she was a Super Bowl champion and feeling good. It's hard to be angry with such good vibes percolating all around and even inside her. But instead of releasing an expletive-laced tirade that ended with spitting in his face, Traci smiled, and said, "I look forward to that day."

Tip smiled, and replied, "Thank you."

Tip gave Shawn an upward nod with a slight smile and

Shawn returned the up nod sans smile. Tip gave Billie and Branson a down nod of acknowledgement and they both did the same. He then left on the road to begin his journey towards becoming a better man.

At that moment confetti rained down from the sky. Cleo stepped onto the podium with the Lombardi Trophy in hand. "Wow…what a season Detroit! This team standing up here with me tonight."

Cleo looked around and noticed Traci, Shawn, Billie, and Branson on the field engaged in conversation, "What are you doing down there, get up here." They hurried to the podium as Cleo waved her hands like a traffic cop when the lights worked and there was no real traffic. Once they were in position, Cleo continued, "This team standing up here with me tonight has faced challenges both on and off the field. Victory isn't all about winning. It's about the hearts you've managed to change along the way. Without further ado…"

EPILOGUE

"Football is a game of inches, and inches make champions."
~Vince Lombardi Jr., Head Coach Green Bay Packers

The celebration went on till the wee hours of the morning at Ford Field. Job and Disney somehow managed to stay up most of the night, but as the sun crossed Disney's half-open eyes, Job knew the sleep monster would soon win the battle. At least as far as Disney was concerned. Her eyes grew heavy and soon she fell asleep on one of the benches in the suite.

Still buzzing from the high of the unexpected victory, sleep didn't reach Job so easily. *Where's my phone?* He spotted Shawn asleep on the opposite sofa holding both his and Job's phones in his hands. Job smiled as he gently removed his phone from his father's grasp.

Job went to IG so he could like some of the posts about the Lions' victory. Before he could scroll through his feed, he noticed he had a DM. He debated whether or not to open it because sometimes you just didn't know what you might find. Feeling lucky, he clicked the arrow to check it. As he read the message, he fell back. Fortunately, there was a chair waiting behind him to break his fall. Three words, make that four if you count the sender, were enough to make him break out in a cold sweat and rattle his pounding heart like a bass drum.

Had a bet with my mother. But first we had to get them there.
-Eli

Job didn't expect to get an answer. If he did get one, it wouldn't be a straight answer. But might as well take a chance.

What was the bet, Eli?

If you made someone think they had a chance, would they take that chance and prove that they always had what it took. I lost.

Are you serious? So it was all them? They did this on their own?

We would ACCOMPLISH many more things if we did not think of them as IMPOSSIBLE, Job. Anyway, I'll be seeing you. Triple or nothing.

"Job, what are you doing?"

Disney's voice startled Job and he almost dropped his phone. Nervously, he answered "Just scrolling through IG."

Job went back to read the message, but it was gone. *Where did it go?*

Disney stood up and stretched. "Let's find some food."

Job hesitated. Double or nothing? Was the game working again? Would it start all over again? He had to check! He needed to know! He needed to go home now! He had to stop the game now! His mind created scenarios that were not based in fact. He worried about trades, signings, drafts, coaches, teams relocating. What if the game became more entrenched... more powerful? This was a new level. Anything was possible.

He needed to leave, but there was no way he could do that without raising Disney's suspicions. If he didn't stop it now, Job did not even want to consider what the game might do next. Job tossed his phone and grabbed Disney's hand. He would have to wait until, at least until breakfast was over, to go home and find out the future of himself, Disney, Shawn, his new family and the entire NFL.

The National Football League. It was truly something special. As he looked at Disney, he thought about how it had brought them together and torn them apart. The outcome of so many games was truly decided by inches. One inch to the right and Branson doesn't catch that pass. One inch too high and Shawn doesn't get that first down. One inch to the left and Traci doesn't hit that pylon. Football was truly a game of inches, and so was love. Love too could be influenced by the simplest decisions or subtlest changes. With that thought, Job stared into Disney's eyes and caressed her cheek. Disney placed her hand under his chin. It was impossible to determine who initiated it but it was clear that they both decided that it was well past time to close the distance, the inches between them... with a blitz.

ABOUT THE TEAM

Demetrius Jones, Esq., MBA
Author
demetriusjones.com
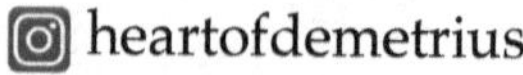 heartofdemetrius

DC Hicks
Author
readwithdc@gmail.com

Dr. Erin Macri, Ph.d
Editor
@Erin_Macri

Tanya Maifat
Designer
tmaifat@gmail.com

www.ingramcontent.com/pod-product-compliance
Lightning Source LLC
Chambersburg PA
CBHW021221220726

48287CB00016B/2229